THE PELICAN SHAKESPEARE

GENERAL EDITOR ALFRED HARBAGE

ROMEO AND JULIET

WILLIAM SHAKESPEARE

ROMEO AND
JULIET

EDITED BY JOHN E. HANKINS

PENGUIN BOOKS

PENGUIN BOOKS
Published by the Penguin Group
Penguin Books USA Inc.,
375 Hudson Street, New York, New York 10014, U.S.A.
Penguin Books Ltd, 27 Wrights Lane, London W8 5TZ, England
Penguin Books Australia Ltd, Ringwood, Victoria, Australia
Penguin Books Canada Ltd, 10 Alcorn Avenue,
Toronto, Ontario, Canada M4V 3B2
Penguin Books (N.Z.) Ltd, 182–190 Wairau Road,
Auckland 10, New Zealand

Penguin Books Ltd, Registered Offices:
Harmondsworth, Middlesex, England

First published in *The Pelican Shakespeare* 1960
This revised edition first published 1970

33   35   34   32

Copyright © Penguin Books, Inc., 1960, 1970
Copyright renewed John E. Hankins, 1988
All rights reserved

Library of Congress catalog card number: 70-98368
ISBN 0 14 071419 7

Printed in the United States of America
Set in Monotype Ehrhardt

CONTENTS

PUBLISHER'S NOTE

Soon after the thirty-eight volumes forming *The Pelican Shakespeare* had been published, they were brought together in *The Complete Pelican Shakespeare*. The editorial revisions and new textual features are explained in detail in the General Editor's Preface to the one-volume edition. They have all been incorporated in the present volume. The following should be mentioned in particular:

The lines are not numbered in arbitrary units. Instead all lines are numbered which contain a word, phrase, or allusion explained in the glossarial notes. In the occasional instances where there is a long stretch of unannotated text, certain lines are numbered in italics to serve the conventional reference purpose.

The intrusive and often inaccurate place-headings inserted by early editors are omitted (as is becoming standard practise), but for the convenience of those who miss them, an indication of locale now appears as first item in the annotation of each scene.

In the interest of both elegance and utility, each speech-prefix is set in a separate line when the speaker's lines are in verse, except when these words form the second half of a pentameter line. Thus the verse form of the speech is kept visually intact, and turned-over lines are avoided. What is printed as verse and what is printed as prose has, in general, the authority of the original texts. Departures from the original texts in this regard have only the authority of editorial tradition and the judgment of the Pelican editors; and, in a few instances, are admittedly arbitrary.

SHAKESPEARE AND
HIS STAGE

William Shakespeare was christened in Holy Trinity Church, Stratford-upon-Avon, April 26, 1564. His birth is traditionally assigned to April 23. He was the eldest of four boys and two girls who survived infancy in the family of John Shakespeare, glover and trader of Henley Street, and his wife Mary Arden, daughter of a small landowner of Wilmcote. In 1568 John was elected Bailiff (equivalent to Mayor) of Stratford, having already filled the minor municipal offices. The town maintained for the sons of the burgesses a free school, taught by a university graduate and offering preparation in Latin sufficient for university entrance; its early registers are lost, but there can be little doubt that Shakespeare received the formal part of his education in this school.

On November 27, 1582, a license was issued for the marriage of William Shakespeare (aged eighteen) and Ann Hathaway (aged twenty-six), and on May 26, 1583, their child Susanna was christened in Holy Trinity Church. The inference that the marriage was forced upon the youth is natural but not inevitable; betrothal was legally binding at the time, and was sometimes regarded as conferring conjugal rights. Two additional children of the marriage, the twins Hamnet and Judith, were christened on February 2, 1585. Meanwhile the prosperity of the elder Shakespeares had declined, and William was impelled to seek a career outside Stratford.

The tradition that he spent some time as a country

teacher is old but unverifiable. Because of the absence of records his early twenties are called the "lost years," and only one thing about them is certain – that at least some of these years were spent in winning a place in the acting profession. He may have begun as a provincial trouper, but by 1592 he was established in London and prominent enough to be attacked. In a pamphlet of that year, *Groats-worth of Wit*, the ailing Robert Greene complained of the neglect which university writers like himself had suffered from actors, one of whom was daring to set up as a playwright:

… an vpstart Crow, beautified with our feathers, that with his *Tygers hart wrapt in a Players hyde*, supposes he is as well able to bombast out a blanke verse as the best of you: and beeing an absolute *Iohannes fac totum*, is in his owne conceit the onely Shake-scene in a countrey.

The pun on his name, and the parody of his line "O tiger's heart wrapped in a woman's hide". (*3 Henry VI*), pointed clearly to Shakespeare. Some of his admirers protested, and Henry Chettle, the editor of Greene's pamphlet, saw fit to apologize:

… I am as sory as if the originall fault had beene my fault, because my selfe haue seene his demeanor no lesse ciuill than he excelent in the qualitie he professes : Besides, diuers of worship haue reported his vprightnes of dealing, which argues his honesty, and his facetious grace in writting, that approoues his Art. (Prefatory epistle, *Kind-Harts Dreame*)

The plague closed the London theatres for many months in 1592–94, denying the actors their livelihood. To this period belong Shakespeare's two narrative poems, *Venus and Adonis* and *The Rape of Lucrece*, both dedicated to the Earl of Southampton. No doubt the poet was rewarded with a gift of money as usual in such cases, but he did no further dedicating and we have no reliable information on whether Southampton, or anyone else, became his regular patron. His sonnets, first mentioned in 1598 and published without his consent in 1609, are intimate without being

8

explicitly autobiographical. They seem to commemorate the poet's friendship with an idealized youth, rivalry with a more favored poet, and love affair with a dark mistress; and his bitterness when the mistress betrays him in conjunction with the friend; but it is difficult to decide precisely what the "story" is, impossible to decide whether it is fictional or true. The true distinction of the sonnets, at least of those not purely conventional, rests in the universality of the thoughts and moods they express, and in their poignancy and beauty.

In 1594 was formed the theatrical company known until 1603 as the Lord Chamberlain's men, thereafter as the King's men. Its original membership included, besides Shakespeare, the beloved clown Will Kempe and the famous actor Richard Burbage. The company acted in various London theatres and even toured the provinces, but it is chiefly associated in our minds with the Globe Theatre built on the south bank of the Thames in 1599. Shakespeare was an actor and joint owner of this company (and its Globe) through the remainder of his creative years. His plays, written at the average rate of two a year, together with Burbage's acting won it its place of leadership among the London companies.

Individual plays began to appear in print, in editions both honest and piratical, and the publishers became increasingly aware of the value of Shakespeare's name on the title pages. As early as 1598 he was hailed as the leading English dramatist in the *Palladis Tamia* of Francis Meres

As *Plautus* and *Seneca* are accounted the best for Comedy and Tragedy among the Latines, so *Shakespeare* among the English is the most excellent in both kinds for the stage: for Comedy, witnes his *Gentlemen of Verona*, his *Errors*, his *Loue labors lost*, his *Loue labours wonne* [at one time in print but no longer extant, at least under this title], his *Midsummers night dream*, & his *Merchant of Venice*; for Tragedy, his *Richard the 2*, *Richard the 3*, *Henry the 4*, *King Iohn*, *Titus Andronicus*, and his *Romeo and Iuliet*.

The note is valuable both in indicating Shakespeare's prestige and in helping us to establish a chronology. In the second half of his writing career, history plays gave place to the great tragedies; and farces and light comedies gave place to the problem plays and symbolic romances. In 1623, seven years after his death, his former fellow-actors, John Heminge and Henry Condell, cooperated with a group of London printers in bringing out his plays in collected form. The volume is generally known as the First Folio.

Shakespeare had never severed his relations with Stratford. His wife and children may sometimes have shared his London lodgings, but their home was Stratford. His son Hamnet was buried there in 1596, and his daughters Susanna and Judith were married there in 1607 and 1616 respectively. (His father, for whom he had secured a coat of arms and thus the privilege of writing himself gentleman, died in 1601, his mother in 1608.) His considerable earnings in London, as actor-sharer, part owner of the Globe, and playwright, were invested chiefly in Stratford property. In 1597 he purchased for £60 New Place, one of the two most imposing residences in the town. A number of other business transactions, as well as minor episodes in his career, have left documentary records. By 1611 he was in a position to retire, and he seems gradually to have withdrawn from theatrical activity in order to live in Stratford. In March, 1616, he made a will, leaving token bequests to Burbage, Heminge, and Condell, but the bulk of his estate to his family. The most famous feature of the will, the bequest of the second-best bed to his wife, reveals nothing about Shakespeare's marriage; the quaintness of the provision seems commonplace to those familiar with ancient testaments. Shakespeare died April 23, 1616, and was buried in the Stratford church where he had been christened. Within seven years a monument was erected to his memory on the north wall of the chancel. Its portrait bust and the Droeshout engraving on the title page of the First Folio provide the only likenesses with an established claim to authenticity. The best verbal vignette was written by his rival Ben Jonson, the more impressive for being imbedded in a context mainly critical:

. . . I loved the man, and doe honour his memory (on this side idolatry) as much as any. Hee was indeed honest, and of an open and free nature: had an excellent Phantsie, brave notions, and gentle expressions. . . . (*Timber or Discoveries*, ca. 1623–30)

*

The reader of Shakespeare's plays is aided by a general knowledge of the way in which they were staged. The King's men acquired a roofed and artificially lighted theatre only toward the close of Shakespeare's career, and then only for winter use. Nearly all his plays were designed for performance in such structures as the Globe – a three-tiered amphitheatre with a large rectangular platform extending to the center of its yard. The plays were staged by daylight, by large casts brilliantly costumed, but with only a minimum of properties, without scenery, and quite possibly without intermissions. There was a rear stage gallery for action "above," and a curtained rear recess for "discoveries" and other special effects, but by far the major portion of any play was enacted upon the projecting platform, with episode following episode in swift succession, and with shifts of time and place signaled the audience only by the momentary clearing of the stage between the episodes. Information about the identity of the characters and, when necessary, about the time and place of the action was incorporated in the dialogue. No place-headings have been inserted in the present editions; these are apt to obscure the original fluidity of structure, with the emphasis upon action and speech rather than scenic background. (Indications of place are supplied in the foot-notes.) The acting, including that of the youthful apprentices to the profession who performed the parts of women, was highly skillful, with a premium placed upon grace of gesture and beauty of diction. The audiences, a cross section of the general public, commonly numbered a thousand, sometimes more than two thousand. Judged by the type of plays they applauded, these audiences were not only large but also perceptive.

THE TEXTS OF THE PLAYS

About half of Shakespeare's plays appeared in print for the first time in the folio volume of 1623. The others had been published individually, usually in quarto volumes, during his lifetime or in the six years following his death. The copy used by the printers of the quartos varied greatly in merit, sometimes representing Shakespeare's true text, sometimes only a debased version of that text. The copy used by the printers of the folio also varied in merit, but was chosen with care. Since it consisted of the best available manuscripts, or the more acceptable quartos (although frequently in editions other than the first), or of quartos corrected by reference to manuscripts, we have good or reasonably good texts of most of the thirty-seven plays.

In the present series, the plays have been newly edited from quarto or folio texts, depending, when a choice offered, upon which is now regarded by bibliographical specialists as the more authoritative. The ideal has been to reproduce the chosen texts with as few alterations as possible, beyond occasional relineation, expansion of abbreviations, and modernization of punctuation and spelling. Emendation is held to a minimum, and such material as has been added, in the way of stage directions and lines supplied by an alternative text, has been enclosed in square brackets.

None of the plays printed in Shakespeare's lifetime were divided into acts and scenes, and the inference is that the author's own manuscripts were not so divided. In the folio collection, some of the plays remained undivided, some were divided into acts, and some were divided into acts and scenes. During the eighteenth century all of the plays were divided into acts and scenes, and in the Cambridge edition of the mid-nineteenth century, from which the influential Globe text derived, this division was more or less regularized and the lines were numbered. Many useful works of reference employ the act–scene–line apparatus thus established.

Since this act–scene division is obviously convenient, but is of very dubious authority so far as Shakespeare's own structural principles are concerned, or the original manner of staging his plays, a problem is presented to modern editors. In the present series the act–scene division is retained marginally, and may be viewed as a reference aid like the line numbering. A star marks the points of division when these points have been determined by a cleared stage indicating a shift of time and place in the action of the play, or when no harm results from the editorial assumption that there is such a shift. However, at those points where the established division is clearly misleading – that is, where continuous action has been split up into separate "scenes" – the star is omitted and the distortion corrected. This mechanical expedient seemed the best means of combining utility and accuracy.

THE GENERAL EDITOR

INTRODUCTION

Romeo and Juliet is a play of young love. No other conveys so well the impetuous, idealistic passion of youth. The hero and heroine are not remarkable except in the overwhelming strength of their love for each other. Readers who love deeply may find here the idealized utterance of their feelings, and those who do not love deeply are led to wish that they could. The universal longing for a perfect romantic love, for the union of physical desire with selfless self-surrender, finds full expression in this play and makes it what Georg Brandes has called the great typical love-tragedy of the world.

That this appeal to a universal longing in human nature is the true secret of the play's success is witnessed by the great popularity of the balcony scene in Act II, which is not at all the dramatic climax of the play but is usually the scene most clearly remembered. In former centuries the Library of Oxford University kept its folio copy of Shakespeare's works chained to a desk at which students could stand and read. The well-thumbed pages of the balcony scene and of the parting scene in Act III give mute evidence that for young Oxonians these utterances of love were the most popular passages in all of Shakespeare's works.

Indeed, Shakespeare's finest achievement in this play is the successful portrayal of passionate physical love in terms of purity and innocence. The suggestive wink and the salacious leer are present in the jestings of the Nurse and the innuendoes of Mercutio, but these merely serve as contrasts to what Romeo and Juliet feel within themselves. When Juliet, soliloquizing, expresses her eager anticipation of her wedding night, she does not appear immodest but innocent in the best sense. Her passion for Romeo is ennobling, and the same is true of Romeo's love for her. The completeness of their devotion to each other leads them to ironic, untimely death; yet we cannot feel that this is wholly a defeat, for their love has risen superior to the storms of circumstance. In the words of Professor van Kranendonk, late of Amsterdam: "The poet has placed this springtime love in so intense a poetic light that an afterglow still remains over the somber ending. When we hear the names of Romeo and Juliet, we do not think first of all (as with Othello and Desdemona) about their pain, their misery, and their terrible undoing, but about their happiness together."

In style and manner, *Romeo and Juliet* seems nearer to *A Midsummer Night's Dream* than to Shakespeare's other plays. One finds the same intense lyricism, the same dependence upon rhymed couplets, the same enchantment of moonlight scenes, and the same interest in fairy lore. Finally, in *A Midsummer Night's Dream* there occurs a passage which seems to contain the theme enlarged upon in *Romeo and Juliet*. Lysander laments that in stories of the past the "course of true love never did run smooth" and that mutual happiness seldom endured, passing like a sound, a shadow, a dream, a flash of lightning swallowed up in darkness. "So quick bright things come to confusion," Lysander concludes, to which Hermia replies, "If then true lovers have been ever crossed, / It stands as an edict in destiny." These lines anticipate the "star-crossed lovers" of the Prologue to *Romeo and Juliet* and suggest that the evanescence of "bright things," particularly of young love, is a key to the mood in which the later play was written.

For some years scholars have debated the relative dates

of these two plays. Internal evidence, while indicating 1594–95 as the date of *A Midsummer Night's Dream*, seemed to place *Romeo and Juliet* in 1591. In the Nurse's first scene, she says, "'Tis since the earthquake now eleven years," a line which has the earmarks of a topical allusion. If she refers to the much-publicized earthquake which shook England on April 6, 1580, then the play should be dated in 1591, a date which on other grounds seems much too early. Recent scholarship, however, has given us a choice of earthquakes, since one occurred in Dorsetshire in 1583 and one in Kent in 1585. A "terrible earthquake" which occurred on the Continent on March 1, 1584, is described in William Covell's *Polimanteia* (1595), a book which also praised "Sweet Shakspeare." It is therefore obvious that the earthquake could date *Romeo and Juliet* in 1594, 1595, or 1596, just as well as in 1591.

Other methods of establishing the date have been attempted. The play opens "a fortnight and odd days" before Lammas Tide (August 1). Calculating the position of the moon as described in the play yields 1596 as the only year that will fit astronomically. The first edition of the play, the quarto of 1597, is described on the title page as having been acted by "Lord Hunsdon's servants." Shakespeare's company was known by this title only from July 1596 to March 1597. A scholar who has compared the type face of this edition with other books issued by its printer, John Danter, concludes that the quarto was printed in February or March of 1597. Since it was a reported edition and was presumably not authorized by Shakespeare, it probably represented an attempt to exploit the popularity of a new play. We may therefore with some confidence assign the composition of the play to the middle of 1596, in which case the earthquake recalled by the Nurse would be the one which occurred in Kent on August 4, 1585. The play followed *A Midsummer Night's Dream* by slightly more than a year.

Shakespeare's source for this play was *The Tragicall Historye of Romeus and Iuliet, written first in Italian by Bandell, and now in Englishe by Ar. Br.* (1562). This work by Arthur Broke, or Brooke, is a long narrative poem based on the prose of Bandello (1554) through an intermediate French version by Pierre Boaistuau (1559). Before Bandello, elements of the story were used by Luigi da Porto (1525) and Masuccio Salernitano (1476). Brooke's poem apparently created in England a vogue for "tragical histories" translated from Bandello, Boccaccio, and other prose romancers. In the two decades following 1562, extensive collections of these were published in prose by William Painter, Geoffrey Fenton, and George Pettie, and in verse by James Sandford, George Turbervile, Robert Smyth, and Richard Tarleton. Painter's work included a prose translation of the Romeo–Juliet story, but Shakespeare seems not to have used it. Brooke tells us in his preface that he had recently seen a play on the same subject acted on the stage (probably at the Inns of Court), but it seems unlikely that this play came to Shakespeare's attention thirty years later, since no further performances or printings of it are recorded. His obvious source, and probably his only one, was Brooke's poem.

Shakespeare's dramatic genius may be studied in the changes which he has made from Brooke's narrative. He has shortened the duration of the action from nine months to less than a week. Thus the hasty march of events becomes a major cause of the tragedy; there is not time to settle problems which greater leisure would have simplified. He has expanded Mercutio's role from a mere reference in Brooke and has invented the two duels involving Tybalt, thereby enhancing Romeo's dilemma of love against honor; for in Brooke's poem Romeo kills Tybalt accidentally while defending himself in a street brawl. He has taken from Brooke almost every incident involving the Nurse, yet he has created in her affectionate, vulgar, easygoing personality one of his most original characters. Finally, he has portrayed in the Capulet household a remarkable study in family psychology.

In Bandello's story Juliet is eighteen years old, in Brooke's poem she is sixteen, and in Shakespeare's play she is nearing her fourteenth birthday. Since Renaissance physiologists generally considered fourteen to mark the beginning of puberty (cf. *The Winter's Tale*, II, i, 147), Shakespeare apparently intended to picture Juliet's love for Romeo as first love, strengthened by the fact that she is just becoming emotionally aware of the meaning of love itself. (A similar purpose is evident in *The Tempest*, where Miranda is approximately the same age as Juliet.) In her emotions Juliet has suddenly become a woman, while in other respects she is still a child. Neither she nor her parents can quite understand this change; they consider her refusal to marry Paris childish willfulness, and she is too much in awe of them to tell them the truth.

Capulet is an old man married to a young woman. In spite of Lady Capulet's reference to her "old age," she is twenty-eight, only twice the age of her daughter. Capulet, however, had last attended a masquerade more than thirty years before and is now probably in his sixties. Since the earth had "swallowèd all my hopes" but Juliet, and since she is the only child born to Lady Capulet, Capulet must have had children by a former marriage. Lady Capulet has retained something of the awe of the child-bride for her older husband and defers to his judgment – and to his temper – in hastening the marriage with Paris. Her habit of deference to his wishes may have caused her to withhold from Juliet sympathy which she normally would have given. Capulet assumes the management of the household duties and dearly loves to plan big parties. Even among his laments for Juliet's death is a regret that it should "murder our solemnity," i.e., spoil the feast which he had planned. His domestic ménage is hardly that of a great Italian nobleman and perhaps more nearly resembles that of a wealthy burgher of Stratford, recalled from Shakespeare's youth.

The play also represents an advance in Shakespeare's ability to reproduce the language of young gentlemen. The badinage of Mercutio, Romeo, and Benvolio is a decided improvement over similar conversations in earlier plays. Mercutio's unique blend of critical acumen, delicate fancy, and obscene levity makes him a remarkable character creation. One critic suggests that Shakespeare was forced to kill Mercutio lest he "steal the show" from the major figures of the plot. Like Jaques and Falstaff in later plays, he exists more as a character portrayed for its own innate interest than as an essential participant in the dramatic action.

Unlike Shakespeare's later tragedies, *Romeo and Juliet* is a play of externals, of characters portrayed in their relationships with each other. Their motives and feelings are readily understandable. There is a minimum of introspective brooding, enigmatic utterance, and puzzlement over moral problems; instead, all is quick decision and rapid action. In later tragedies Shakespeare undertook to explore the secret recesses of the soul, but here he shows people in conflict with external circumstance. Their errors of judgment are not errors involving a consciousness of sin but are attributable to impetuous haste and unkind fate. Nothing is withheld from the reader; characters and their motives are revealed as completely as possible. The same lack of reticence is evident in the literary style, which abounds in conceits, plays on words, and luxuriant poetic descriptions. Perhaps it is the quality of complete representations of emotions and moods that has made the play a favorite with musical composers: Gounod, Berlioz, Tchaikovsky, Prokofiev, and Milhaud, among others.

In *Romeo and Juliet* Shakespeare exploits dramatic irony in abrupt reversals of situation. Romeo, despondent, goes unwillingly to Capulet's ball and is quickly raised to joy by his encounter with Juliet, only to find that she is his hereditary enemy. This obstacle overcome, his joy reaches a height with his wedding, but within a half hour he is plunged into despair after his duel with Tybalt. At the beginning of Act V, Romeo is cheerful because of a dream which seems to foretell his reunion with Juliet, but his hopes are quickly dashed by Balthasar's news of her death. The supreme instance of irony comes as he stands beside her in the sepulchre, observing that she looks as though alive, and then drinks the poison to join her in death. The audience knows that she really is alive and will awake in a few minutes. In David Garrick's acting version of the play (as in Bandello's story) Juliet awakes before Romeo dies, and he thus realizes the bitter irony of his situation. The questionable dramatic propriety of this ending has caused considerable debate among students of the play.

Shakespeare makes one other effective use of irony. When Capulet and his wife are scolding Juliet for her refusal to marry Paris, each petulantly expresses a wish for her death. "I would the fool were married to her grave," says Lady Capulet. Capulet says that they have only one child, "But now I see this one is one too much." They do not intend these statements seriously, as Juliet doubtless realizes, but their words are ominous of what is to come. They get what they ask for.

In recent years numerous attempts have been made to state a central theme for the play. One critic views it as a tragedy of unawareness. Capulet and Montague are unaware of the fateful issues which may hang upon their quarrel. Romeo and Juliet fall in love while unaware that they are hereditary enemies. Mercutio and Tybalt are both unaware of the true state of affairs when they fight their duel. In the chain of events leading to the final tragedy, even the servants play a part and are unaware of the results of their actions. The final scene, with Friar Laurence's long explanation, is dramatically justified because it brings Montague, Capulet, Lady Capulet, and the Prince to at least a partial awareness of their responsibility for what has happened. Supplementing this view of the play is one which finds it to be a study of the wholeness and complexity of things in human affairs. The issues of the feud may appear to be simple and clear, but in reality they are highly complex, giving rise to results which are completely unforeseen. The goodness or badness of human actions is relative, not absolute, an idea symbolically set forth in Friar Laurence's opening speech on herbs which are medicinal or poisonous according to the manner of their use.

Other clues to the meaning of the play may be found in the repetitive imagery employed by Shakespeare. The images of haste, of events rushing to a conclusion, are found throughout. When Romeo says, "I stand on sudden haste," Friar Laurence answers, "They stumble that run fast," and thus expresses one moral to be drawn from the play. Romeo and Mercutio symbolize their wit-combat by the wild-goose chase, a reckless cross-country horse race. "Swits and spurs," cries Romeo, using the imagery of speed. Numerous other instances may be found.

Closely allied to the imagery of haste is the violence expressed in the gunpowder image. The Friar warns that too impetuous love is like fire and powder, which, "as they kiss, consume." Romeo desires a poison that will expel life from his body, like powder fired from a cannon. This may identify the Apothecary's poison as aconite, since elsewhere Shakespeare compares the action of aconite with that of "rash gunpowder" (*2 Henry IV*, IV, iv, 48). Violence is also expressed in the image of shipwreck which may end the voyage of life. Capulet compares Juliet weeping to a bark in danger from tempests. Romeo describes his death as the shipwreck of his "seasick weary bark." Earlier, after expressing a premonition that attendance at Capulet's party will cause his death, he resigns himself to him "that hath the steerage of my course," anticipating his later images of the ship and the voyage of life.

Also repeated in the play is the image of Death as the lover of Juliet. She herself uses it, her father uses it beside her bier, and Romeo uses it most effectively in the final scene. The effect of this repeated image is to suggest that Juliet is foredoomed to die, that Death, personified, has claimed her for his own. It thus strengthens the ominous note of fate which is felt throughout the play.

That *Romeo and Juliet* is a tragedy of fate can hardly be doubted. Shakespeare says as much in the Prologue. The lovers are marked for death; their fortunes are "crossed" by the stars. The reason for their doom is likewise given: only the shock of their deaths can force their parents to end the senseless feud. At the end of the play Capulet calls the lovers "Poor sacrifices of our enmity," and the Prince describes their deaths as Heaven's punishment of their parents' hate. Romeo's premonition of death before going to the party attributes it to some "consequence yet hanging in the stars." The note of fate is struck repeatedly during the play. "A greater power than we can contradict / Hath thwarted our intents," says Friar Laurence to Juliet in the tomb. The numerous mischances experienced by the lovers are not fortuitous bad luck but represent the working out of some hidden design. Critics who attack the play for lacking inevitability have misunderstood Shakespeare's dramatic technique. Like Hamlet's adventure with the pirates, the sequence of mishaps here is deliberately made so improbable that chance alone cannot explain it. Fate, or the will of Heaven, must be invoked.

One finds it difficult to interpret this tragedy in Aristotelian terms, since the parents are really the ones who have the "tragic flaw" and suffer the results of their folly, as Lear does, in the deaths of their children. Yet the children, not the parents, are the major figures of the play. Some critics have named impetuosity as Romeo's "tragic flaw," but Romeo is less impetuous than Tybalt or Mercutio, and one can hardly name as a "flaw" a quality which is pictured as common to youth. It is true that greater placidity of temperament and more deliberate speed might have averted the tragedy under the given circumstances, yet the pattern of circumstances might easily have been different and the will of fate accomplished just the same.

Shakespeare makes it clear that society is partly responsible for the tragedy. The feud between noble families was a matter of social convention. So was the necessity to take personal revenge for an insult to one's honor. Here there seems to be a topical allusion. Prince Escalus represents the view of Queen Elizabeth, whose government decreed that homicide in a duel should be punishable as murder. She was determined to stamp out duelling. Furthermore, the evil arising from any form of civil strife is a constantly reiterated theme in Elizabethan literature. Current social attitudes may be noted both in the Prince's edict against street fighting and in the cavalier disregard of it.

As might be expected, *Romeo and Juliet* has been a popular stage play, never more so than now, when each year sees from ten to twenty new productions by professional and amateur groups. What Hamlet is for the actor, Juliet is for the actress, a role which offers the fullest scope for the display of female histrionics. In past centuries Mrs Betterton and Fanny Kemble made great successes in the part. In the present century Julia Marlowe, Eva Le Gallienne, Jane Cowl, and Katherine Cornell are among those who have played Juliet. The producer of this play always has a problem, for very few great actresses achieve eminence by the age of fourteen, and most of them are recognizably mature women trying to look young. To a lesser extent the same problem exists in casting the masculine roles. The producer must choose between the verisimilitude of a youthful cast and the more sophisticated acting of experienced players. Nevertheless, despite all difficulties, *Romeo and Juliet* is still constantly staged with success, and most of us can recall productions in which it proved as vivid and moving in the theatre as it always proves on the printed page.

University of Maine   JOHN E. HANKINS

NOTE ON THE TEXT

An abridged and inaccurate version of *Romeo and Juliet*, evidently "reporting" the play in performance, was published in quarto in 1597. In 1599 appeared a good quarto, probably printed from Shakespeare's draft with some reference to the earlier quarto. A third quarto was printed from the second in 1609, and this was used as copy for the fourth quarto (1622?) and the text of the first folio, 1623. The present edition follows the quarto of 1599, with faulty readings corrected with caution by reference to the quarto of 1597, and with few emendations. (All material departures from the text of the 1599 quarto are listed in an appendix, with the exception of added stage directions and adjusted cancellations; the two latter classes of departure are noted as they occur.) None of the early texts, including that of the folio, are divided into acts and scenes. The division supplied marginally in the present edition is "editorial" and is for purposes of reference only.

ROMEO AND JULIET

[NAMES OF THE ACTORS

Chorus
Escalus, Prince of Verona
Paris, a young count, kinsman to the Prince
Montague
Capulet
An old Man, of the Capulet family
Romeo, son to Montague
Mercutio, kinsman to the Prince, and friend to Romeo
Benvolio, nephew to Montague, and friend to Romeo
Tybalt, nephew to Lady Capulet
Friar Laurence }
Friar John } *Franciscans*
Balthasar, servant to Romeo
Abram, servant to Montague
Sampson }
Gregory } *servants to Capulet*
Peter, servant to Juliet's nurse
An Apothecary
Three Musicians
An Officer
Lady Montague, wife to Montague
Lady Capulet, wife to Capulet
Juliet, daughter to Capulet
Nurse to Juliet
*Citizens of Verona, Gentlemen and Gentlewomen of both
    houses, Maskers, Torchbearers, Pages, Guards,
    Watchmen, Servants, and Attendants*

Scene: *Verona, Mantua*]

ROMEO AND JULIET

[Enter] Chorus.

CHORUS

Two households, both alike in dignity,
  In fair Verona, where we lay our scene,
From ancient grudge break to new mutiny,   3
  Where civil blood makes civil hands unclean.   4
From forth the fatal loins of these two foes
  A pair of star-crossed lovers take their life ;   6
Whose misadventured piteous overthrows
  Doth with their death bury their parents' strife.
The fearful passage of their death-marked love,   9
  And the continuance of their parents' rage,
Which, but their children's end, naught could remove,
  Is now the two hours' traffic of our stage ;   12
The which if you with patient ears attend,
What here shall miss, our toil shall strive to mend.
                           [Exit.]

Pro. **3** *mutiny* outbursts of violence   **4** *civil . . . civil* citizens' . . . fellow citizens' **6** *star-crossed* thwarted by adverse stars **9** *death-marked* foredoomed to death   **12** *two . . . stage* our stage-business for the next two hours

I, i   *Enter Sampson and Gregory, with swords and*
       bucklers, of the house of Capulet.

1 SAMPSON Gregory, on my word, we'll not carry coals.

2 GREGORY No, for then we should be colliers.

3 SAMPSON I mean, an we be in choler, we'll draw.

4 GREGORY Ay, while you live, draw your neck out of collar.

SAMPSON I strike quickly, being moved.

GREGORY But thou art not quickly moved to strike.

SAMPSON A dog of the house of Montague moves me.

GREGORY To move is to stir, and to be valiant is to stand.
Therefore, if thou art moved, thou runn'st away.

SAMPSON A dog of that house shall move me to stand. I
11   will take the wall of any man or maid of Montague's.

12 GREGORY That shows thee a weak slave; for the weakest
goes to the wall.

SAMPSON 'Tis true; and therefore women, being the
15   weaker vessels, are ever thrust to the wall. Therefore I
will push Montague's men from the wall and thrust his
maids to the wall.

GREGORY The quarrel is between our masters, and us
their men.

SAMPSON 'Tis all one. I will show myself a tyrant. When
I have fought with the men, I will be cruel with the
maids – I will cut off their heads.

GREGORY The heads of the maids?

SAMPSON Ay, the heads of the maids, or their maiden-
25   heads. Take it in what sense thou wilt.

GREGORY They must take it in sense that feel it.

SAMPSON Me they shall feel while I am able to stand; and
28   'tis known I am a pretty piece of flesh.

29 GREGORY 'Tis well thou art not fish; if thou hadst, thou

I, i A street in Verona **1** *carry coals* i.e. suffer insults **2** *colliers* coal
dealers **3** *an* if; *choler* anger; *draw* draw our swords **4** *collar* hang-
man's noose **11** *take the wall* pass on the inner and cleaner part of the
sidewalk **12–13** *the weakest . . . wall* i.e. is pushed from his place (proverbial) **15** *weaker vessels* (cf. 1 Peter iii, 7) **25–26** *sense . . . sense* meaning
. . . physical sensation **28, 29** *flesh, fish* (alluding to the proverb 'Neither
fish nor flesh')

hadst been poor-John. Draw thy tool! Here comes two 30
of the house of Montagues.

Enter two other Servingmen [Abram and Balthasar].

SAMPSON My naked weapon is out. Quarrel! I will back
thee.

GREGORY How? turn thy back and run?

SAMPSON Fear me not.

GREGORY No, marry. I fear thee! 36

SAMPSON Let us take the law of our sides; let them begin. 37

GREGORY I will frown as I pass by, and let them take it as
they list.

SAMPSON Nay, as they dare. I will bite my thumb at 40
them, which is disgrace to them if they bear it.

ABRAM Do you bite your thumb at us, sir?

SAMPSON I do bite my thumb, sir.

ABRAM Do you bite your thumb at us, sir?

SAMPSON *[aside to Gregory]* Is the law of our side if I say
ay?

GREGORY *[aside to Sampson]* No.

SAMPSON No, sir, I do not bite my thumb at you, sir; but
I bite my thumb, sir.

GREGORY Do you quarrel, sir?

ABRAM Quarrel, sir? No, sir. 50

SAMPSON But if you do, sir, I am for you. I serve as good
a man as you.

ABRAM No better.

SAMPSON Well, sir.

Enter Benvolio.

GREGORY *[aside to Sampson]* Say 'better.' Here comes
one of my master's kinsmen.

SAMPSON Yes, better, sir.

ABRAM You lie.

---

30 *poor-John* dried hake, the cheapest fish; *tool* sword (with ribald innuendo)
36 *marry* indeed (originally an oath by the Virgin Mary); *I fear thee* to
suppose me afraid of you is ridiculous   37 *take . . . of* have the law on
40 *bite my thumb* (an insulting gesture)

SAMPSON Draw, if you be men. Gregory, remember thy
60   swashing blow.
  They fight.
BENVOLIO Part, fools!
 Put up your swords. You know not what you do.
  Enter Tybalt.

TYBALT
63   What, art thou drawn among these heartless hinds?
 Turn thee, Benvolio! look upon thy death.

BENVOLIO
 I do but keep the peace. Put up thy sword,
 Or manage it to part these men with me.

TYBALT
 What, drawn, and talk of peace? I hate the word
 As I hate hell, all Montagues, and thee.
 Have at thee, coward!
  [They fight.]
  Enter [an Officer, and] three or four Citizens with
  clubs or partisans.

70 OFFICER Clubs, bills, and partisans! Strike! beat them
 down!
CITIZENS Down with the Capulets! Down with the
 Montagues!
  Enter old Capulet in his gown, and his Wife.

CAPULET
 What noise is this? Give me my long sword, ho!

WIFE
 A crutch, a crutch! Why call you for a sword?

CAPULET
 My sword, I say! Old Montague is come
76   And flourishes his blade in spite of me.
  Enter old Montague and his Wife.

MONTAGUE
 Thou villain Capulet! – Hold me not, let me go.

---

60 *swashing* smashing **63** *heartless hinds* cowardly servants **70** *bills,
partisans* long-shafted weapons with combined spear-head and cutting-
blade **76** *in spite of* in defiance of

MONTAGUE'S WIFE
>   Thou shalt not stir one foot to seek a foe.
>   *Enter Prince Escalus, with his Train.*

PRINCE
>   Rebellious subjects, enemies to peace,
>   Profaners of this neighbor-stainèd steel –
>   Will they not hear ? What, ho ! you men, you beasts,
>   That quench the fire of your pernicious rage
>   With purple fountains issuing from your veins !
>   On pain of torture, from those bloody hands
>   Throw your mistemp'red weapons to the ground   85
>   And hear the sentence of your movèd prince.
>   Three civil brawls, bred of an airy word   87
>   By thee, old Capulet, and Montague,
>   Have thrice disturbed the quiet of our streets
>   And made Verona's ancient citizens   90
>   Cast by their grave beseeming ornaments   91
>   To wield old partisans, in hands as old,
>   Cank'red with peace, to part your cank'red hate.   93
>   If ever you disturb our streets again,
>   Your lives shall pay the forfeit of the peace.
>   For this time all the rest depart away.
>   You, Capulet, shall go along with me ;
>   And, Montague, come you this afternoon,
>   To know our farther pleasure in this case,
>   To old Freetown, our common judgment place.   100
>   Once more, on pain of death, all men depart.
>   *Exeunt [all but Montague, his Wife, and Benvolio].*

MONTAGUE
>   Who set this ancient quarrel new abroach ?   102
>   Speak, nephew, were you by when it began ?

---

85 *mistemp'red* (1) badly made, (2) used for a bad purpose   87 *airy* made
with breath   90 *ancient citizens* a volunteer guard of older men   91 *grave
beseeming ornaments* staffs and costumes appropriate for the aged   93
Cank'red . . . cank'red rusted . . . malignant   100 *Freetown* (Brooke's
translation of *Villafranca*)   102 *set . . . abroach* reopened this quarrel of
long standing

BENVOLIO

    Here were the servants of your adversary
    And yours, close fighting ere I did approach.
    I drew to part them. In the instant came
    The fiery Tybalt, with his sword prepared;
    Which, as he breathed defiance to my ears,
    He swung about his head and cut the winds,
110   Who, nothing hurt withal, hissed him in scorn.
    While we were interchanging thrusts and blows,
    Came more and more, and fought on part and part,
    Till the Prince came, who parted either part.

MONTAGUE'S WIFE

    O, where is Romeo? Saw you him to-day?
    Right glad I am he was not at this fray.

BENVOLIO

    Madam, an hour before the worshipped sun
    Peered forth the golden window of the East,
    A troubled mind drave me to walk abroad;
    Where, underneath the grove of sycamore
    That westward rooteth from this city side,
    So early walking did I see your son.
122   Towards him I made, but he was ware of me
    And stole into the covert of the wood.
124   I, measuring his affections by my own,
125   Which then most sought where most might not be found,
    Being one too many by my weary self,
    Pursued my humor, not pursuing his,
    And gladly shunned who gladly fled from me.

MONTAGUE

    Many a morning hath he there been seen,
    With tears augmenting the fresh morning's dew,
    Adding to clouds more clouds with his deep sighs;
    But all so soon as the all-cheering sun

---

110 *Who* which; *nothing* not at all; *withal* therewith   122 *ware* aware, wary
124 *affections* inclinations, feelings   125 *most sought . . . found* i.e. desired
solitude

Should in the farthest East begin to draw
The shady curtains from Aurora's bed,   134
Away from light steals home my heavy son   135
And private in his chamber pens himself,
Shuts up his windows, locks fair daylight out,
And makes himself an artificial night.
Black and portentous must this humor prove   139
Unless good counsel may the cause remove.

BENVOLIO
My noble uncle, do you know the cause?

MONTAGUE
I neither know it nor can learn of him.

BENVOLIO
Have you importuned him by any means?

MONTAGUE
Both by myself and many other friends;
But he, his own affections' counsellor,
Is to himself – I will not say how true –
But to himself so secret and so close,
So far from sounding and discovery,   148
As is the bud bit with an envious worm
Ere he can spread his sweet leaves to the air
Or dedicate his beauty to the sun.
Could we but learn from whence his sorrows grow,
We would as willingly give cure as know.
        Enter Romeo.

BENVOLIO
See, where he comes. So please you step aside,
I'll know his grievance, or be much denied.

MONTAGUE
I would thou wert so happy by thy stay
To hear true shrift. Come, madam, let's away.   157
                        Exeunt [Montague and Wife].

134 *Aurora* the dawn   145 *heavy* melancholy   139 *humor* mood   148
sounding being measured (as water-depth is measured with a plummet
line)   157 *shrift* confession

BENVOLIO

158   Good morrow, cousin.

ROMEO   Is the day so young?

BENVOLIO

But new struck nine.

ROMEO   Ay me! sad hours seem long.

Was that my father that went hence so fast?

BENVOLIO

It was. What sadness lengthens Romeo's hours?

ROMEO

Not having that which having makes them short.

BENVOLIO In love?

ROMEO Out–

BENVOLIO Of love?

ROMEO

Out of her favor where I am in love.

BENVOLIO

167   Alas that love, so gentle in his view,

168   Should be so tyrannous and rough in proof!

ROMEO

169   Alas that love, whose view is muffled still,

Should without eyes see pathways to his will!

Where shall we dine? O me! What fray was here?

Yet tell me not, for I have heard it all.

173   Here's much to do with hate, but more with love.

Why then, O brawling love, O loving hate,

O anything, of nothing first create!

O heavy lightness, serious vanity,

Misshapen chaos of well-seeming forms,

Feather of lead, bright smoke, cold fire, sick health,

Still-waking sleep, that is not what it is!

This love feel I, that feel no love in this.

Dost thou not laugh?

---

158 *morrow* morning 167 *view* appearance 168 *in proof* in being ex
perienced 169 *view* sight; *muffled* blindfolded 173–80 *Here's . . . thi*
(the rhetorical name for such paradoxes is oxymoron; cf. III, ii, 73–85)

BENVOLIO   No, coz, I rather weep.   181
ROMEO
Good heart, at what?
BENVOLIO   At thy good heart's oppression.
ROMEO
Why, such is love's transgression.
Griefs of mine own lie heavy in my breast,   184
Which thou wilt propagate, to have it prest
With more of thine. This love that thou hast shown
Doth add more grief to too much of mine own.
Love is a smoke raised with the fume of sighs;
Being purged, a fire sparkling in lovers' eyes;
Being vexed, a sea nourished with lovers' tears.
What is it else? A madness most discreet,
A choking gall, and a preserving sweet.
Farewell, my coz.
BENVOLIO   Soft! I will go along.
An if you leave me so, you do me wrong.
ROMEO
Tut! I have lost myself; I am not here;   195
This is not Romeo, he's some other where.
BENVOLIO
Tell me in sadness, who is that you love?   197
ROMEO
What, shall I groan and tell thee?
BENVOLIO   Groan? Why, no;
But sadly tell me who.
ROMEO
Bid a sick man in sadness make his will.
Ah, word ill urged to one that is so ill!
In sadness, cousin, I do love a woman.
BENVOLIO
I aimed so near when I supposed you loved.

---

181 *coz* cousin   184–87 *Griefs . . . own* your sorrow for my grief grieves me
further to have caused you sorrow   195 *lost* (so both Q2 and Q1, but the
emendation 'left,' has been cogently suggested)   197 *in sadness* seriously

ROMEO

A right good markman. And she's fair I love.

BENVOLIO

205   A right fair mark, fair coz, is soonest hit.

ROMEO

Well, in that hit you miss. She'll not be hit

207   With Cupid's arrow. She hath Dian's wit,

208   And, in strong proof of chastity well armed,

209   From Love's weak childish bow she lives unharmed.

210   She will not stay the siege of loving terms,

Nor bide th' encounter of assailing eyes,

Nor ope her lap to saint-seducing gold.

O, she is rich in beauty ; only poor

214   That, when she dies, with beauty dies her store.

BENVOLIO

215   Then she hath sworn that she will still live chaste ?

ROMEO

216   She hath, and in that sparing makes huge waste ;

For beauty, starved with her severity,

Cuts beauty off from all posterity.

She is too fair, too wise, wisely too fair,

220   To merit bliss by making me despair.

She hath forsworn to love, and in that vow

Do I live dead that live to tell it now.

BENVOLIO

Be ruled by me ; forget to think of her.

ROMEO

O, teach me how I should forget to think !

BENVOLIO

By giving liberty unto thine eyes.

Examine other beauties.

ROMEO   'Tis the way

---

205 *fair mark* bright clean target   207 *Dian* Diana, virgin goddess and huntress   208 *proof* armor   209 *unharmed* (from Q1 ; Q2 reads 'uncharmed,' perhaps correctly)   210–11 *She . . . eyes* i.e. she gives me no chance to woo her   214 *with . . . store* she will leave no children to perpetuate her beauty   215 *still* always   216 *sparing* miserly economy   220 *bliss* heaven

To call hers (exquisite) in question more.   227
These happy masks that kiss fair ladies' brows,
Being black puts us in mind they hide the fair.
He that is strucken blind cannot forget
The precious treasure of his eyesight lost.
Show me a mistress that is passing fair,   232
What doth her beauty serve but as a note
Where I may read who passed that passing fair?
Farewell. Thou canst not teach me to forget.

BENVOLIO
I'll pay that doctrine, or else die in debt.   *Exeunt.* 236

*

Enter Capulet, County Paris, and the Clown   I, ii
[a Servant].

CAPULET
But Montague is bound as well as I,   1
In penalty alike; and 'tis not hard, I think,
For men so old as we to keep the peace.

PARIS
Of honorable reckoning are you both,   4
And pity 'tis you lived at odds so long.
But now, my lord, what say you to my suit?

CAPULET
But saying o'er what I have said before:
My child is yet a stranger in the world,   8
She hath not seen the change of fourteen years;
Let two more summers wither in their pride
Ere we may think her ripe to be a bride.

PARIS
Younger than she are happy mothers made.

227 *in question* to my mind   232 *passing* surpassingly   236 *pay that
doctrine* convince you otherwise
I, ii A street in Verona   1 *bound* under bond   4 *reckoning* reputation   8
world world of society

CAPULET

13 And too soon marred are those so early made.
14 Earth hath swallowèd all my hopes but she;
She is the hopeful lady of my earth.
But woo her, gentle Paris, get her heart;
My will to her consent is but a part.
18 An she agree, within her scope of choice
19 Lies my consent and fair according voice.
20 This night I hold an old accustomed feast,
Whereto I have invited many a guest,
Such as I love; and you among the store,
One more, most welcome, makes my number more.
At my poor house look to behold this night
25 Earth-treading stars that make dark heaven light.
Such comfort as do lusty young men feel
27 When well-apparelled April on the heel
Of limping Winter treads, even such delight
29 Among fresh fennel buds shall you this night
Inherit at my house. Hear all, all see,
And like her most whose merit most shall be;
32 Which, on more view of many, mine, being one,
May stand in number, though in reck'ning none.
Come, go with me.
        [To Servant, giving him a paper]
34   Go, sirrah, trudge about
Through fair Verona; find those persons out
Whose names are written there, and to them say,

---

13 *marred* disfigured by childbirth   14 *hopes* children   18 *scope* range   19 *according* harmoniously agreeing   20 *old accustomed* by custom of long standing   25 *stars* i.e. maidens   27 *April* (Venus' month, the season of lovemaking)   29 *fennel* a flowering herb associated with stimulation and enticement   32–33 *Which . . . none* my daughter will be numerically counted among those present, but possibly not among those you would wish to marry after seeing them all (cf. the common saying 'One is no number')   34 *sirrah* (a familiar form of address, used with servants and sometimes with friends)

My house and welcome on their pleasure stay.

Exit [with Paris].

SERVANT Find them out whose names are written here?
It is written that the shoemaker should meddle with his
yard and the tailor with his last, the fisher with his pen-   40
cil and the painter with his nets; but I am sent to find   41
those persons whose names are here writ, and can never
find what names the writing person hath here writ. I   43
must to the learned. In good time!   44

Enter Benvolio and Romeo.

BENVOLIO
Tut, man, one fire burns out another's burning;   45
  One pain is less'ned by another's anguish;   46
Turn giddy, and be holp by backward turning;   47
  One desperate grief cures with another's languish.
Take thou some new infection to thy eye,   49
And the rank poison of the old will die.

ROMEO
Your plantain leaf is excellent for that.

BENVOLIO
For what, I pray thee?

ROMEO   For your broken shin.

BENVOLIO
Why, Romeo, art thou mad?

ROMEO
Not mad, but bound more than a madman is;   54
Shut up in prison, kept without my food,
Whipped and tormented and – God-den, good fellow.   56

SERVANT God gi' go-den. I pray, sir, can you read?

40, 41 *yard, last, pencil, nets* (occupational tools humorously reversed)   **43**
find find out (since I cannot read)   **44** *In good time* help comes just when I
need it   **45** *one . . . burning* (proverb used often by Shakespeare)   **46**
another's anguish anguish from another pain   **47** *Turn . . . turning* when
giddy from whirling around, be helped by reversing direction   **49** *infection*
(figurately used, but taken literally by Romeo)   **54–56** *bound . . . tormented*
(customary treatment of madmen)   **56** *God-den* good evening (used after
12 noon; cf. II, iv, 105)

ROMEO
Ay, mine own fortune in my misery.

SERVANT Perhaps you have learned it without book. But
I pray, can you read anything you see?

ROMEO
61 Ay, if I know the letters and the language.

SERVANT Ye say honestly. Rest you merry.

ROMEO Stay, fellow; I can read.
He reads the letter.
'Signior Martino and his wife and daughters;
County Anselmo and his beauteous sisters;
The lady widow of Vitruvio;
Signior Placentio and his lovely nieces;
Mercutio and his brother Valentine;
Mine uncle Capulet, his wife, and daughters;
70 My fair niece Rosaline and Livia;
Signior Valentio and his cousin Tybalt;
Lucio and the lively Helena.'
A fair assembly. Whither should they come?

SERVANT Up.

ROMEO Whither? To supper?

SERVANT To our house.

ROMEO Whose house?

SERVANT My master's.

ROMEO
Indeed I should have asked you that before.

SERVANT Now I'll tell you without asking. My master is
the great rich Capulet; and if you be not of the house of
82 Montagues, I pray come and crush a cup of wine. Rest
you merry.   *[Exit.]*

BENVOLIO
At this same ancient feast of Capulet's
Sups the fair Rosaline whom thou so loves;
With all the admirèd beauties of Verona.

---

61 *if I know* (the servant takes this to mean 'only if I have memorized the
appearance of')   **82** *crush* drink

40

Go thither, and with unattainted eye   87
Compare her face with some that I shall show,
And I will make thee think thy swan a crow.

ROMEO
When the devout religion of mine eye
  Maintains such falsehood, then turn tears to fires;
And these, who, often drowned, could never die,   92
  Transparent heretics, be burnt for liars!
One fairer than my love? The all-seeing sun
Ne'er saw her match since first the world begun.

BENVOLIO
Tut! you saw her fair, none else being by,
Herself poised with herself in either eye;
But in that crystal scales let there be weighed   98
Your lady's love against some other maid
That I will show you shining at this feast,
And she shall scant show well that now seems best.   101

ROMEO
I'll go along, no such sight to be shown,
But to rejoice in splendor of my own.   *[Exeunt.]*

*

Enter Capulet's Wife, and Nurse.   I, iii

WIFE
Nurse, where's my daughter? Call her forth to me.

NURSE
Now, by my maidenhead at twelve year old,
I bade her come. What, lamb! what, ladybird!
God forbid, where's this girl? What, Juliet!
        Enter Juliet.

JULIET
How now? Who calls?

87 *unattainted* unprejudiced   92 *these* these eyes; *drowned* i.e. in tears
98 *crystal scales* (Romeo's two eyes are compared to the two ends of a pair of
balances)   101 *scant* scarcely
I, iii Within Capulet's house

NURSE   Your mother.

JULIET   Madam, I am here.
What is your will?

WIFE
7   This is the matter – Nurse, give leave awhile,
        We must talk in secret. Nurse, come back again;
9   I have rememb'red me, thou's hear our counsel.
        Thou knowest my daughter's of a pretty age.

NURSE
        Faith, I can tell her age unto an hour.

WIFE
        She's not fourteen.

NURSE   I'll lay fourteen of my teeth –
13   And yet, to my teen be it spoken, I have but four –
        She's not fourteen. How long is it now
15   To Lammastide?

WIFE   A fortnight and odd days.

NURSE
        Even or odd, of all days in the year,
        Come Lammas Eve at night shall she be fourteen.
        Susan and she (God rest all Christian souls!)
        Were of an age. Well, Susan is with God;
        She was too good for me. But, as I said,
        On Lammas Eve at night shall she be fourteen;
        That shall she, marry; I remember it well.
23   'Tis since the earthquake now eleven years;
        And she was weaned (I never shall forget it),
        Of all the days of the year, upon that day;
        For I had then laid wormwood to my dug,
        Sitting in the sun under the dovehouse wall.
        My lord and you were then at Mantua.
29   Nay, I do bear a brain. But, as I said,
        When it did taste the wormwood on the nipple
        Of my dug and felt it bitter, pretty fool,

7 *give leave* leave us   9 *thou's* thou shalt   13 *teen* sorrow   15 *Lammastide*
August 1   23 *earthquake* (see Introduction)   29 *bear a brain* keep my
mental powers

42

To see it tetchy and fall out with the dug!   32
Shake, quoth the dovehouse! 'Twas no need, I trow,   33
To bid me trudge.   34
And since that time it is eleven years,
For then she could stand high-lone; nay, by th' rood,   36
She could have run and waddled all about;
For even the day before, she broke her brow;
And then my husband (God be with his soul!
'A was a merry man) took up the child.
'Yea,' quoth he, 'dost thou fall upon thy face?
Thou wilt fall backward when thou hast more wit;
Wilt thou not, Jule?' and, by my holidam,   43
The pretty wretch left crying and said 'Ay.'
To see now how a jest shall come about!
I warrant, an I should live a thousand years,
I never should forget it. 'Wilt thou not, Jule?' quoth he,
And, pretty fool, it stinted and said 'Ay.'   48

WIFE
Enough of this. I pray thee hold thy peace.

NURSE
Yes, madam. Yet I cannot choose but laugh
To think it should leave crying and say 'Ay.'
And yet, I warrant, it had upon it brow   52
A bump as big as a young cock'rel's stone;
A perilous knock; and it cried bitterly.
'Yea,' quoth my husband, 'fall'st upon thy face?
Thou wilt fall backward when thou comest to age;
Wilt thou not, Jule?' It stinted and said 'Ay.'

JULIET
And stint thou too, I pray thee, nurse, say I.   58

NURSE
Peace, I have done. God mark thee to his grace!

---

32 *tetchy* fretful **33** *Shake . . . dovehouse* i.e. the dovehouse creaked from the earthquake; *trow* believe **34** *trudge* run away **36** *high-lone* alone; *rood* cross **43** *holidam* halidom, holy relic **48** *stinted* stopped **52** *it brow* its brow **58** *say I* (a pun on 'ay' and 'I'; cf. III, ii, 45–50)

Thou wast the prettiest babe that e'er I nursed.
An I might live to see thee married once,
I have my wish.

WIFE

Marry, that 'marry' is the very theme
I came to talk of. Tell me, daughter Juliet,
How stands your disposition to be married?

JULIET

It is an honor that I dream not of.

NURSE

An honor? Were not I thine only nurse,
I would say thou hadst sucked wisdom from thy teat.

WIFE

Well, think of marriage now. Younger than you,
Here in Verona, ladies of esteem,
Are made already mothers. By my count,
72   I was your mother much upon these years
That you are now a maid. Thus then in brief:
The valiant Paris seeks you for his love.

NURSE

A man, young lady! lady, such a man
76   As all the world – why he's a man of wax.

WIFE

Verona's summer hath not such a flower.

NURSE

Nay, he's a flower, in faith – a very flower.

WIFE

What say you? Can you love the gentleman?
This night you shall behold him at our feast.
Read o'er the volume of young Paris' face,
And find delight writ there with beauty's pen;
83   Examine every married lineament,
And see how one another lends content;

---

72 *much . . . years* at much the same age (indicating that Lady Capulet's age
is now twenty-eight)   76 *a man of wax* handsome, as a wax model   83
married lineament harmonious feature

And what obscured in this fair volume lies   85
Find written in the margent of his eyes.   86
This precious book of love, this unbound lover,
To beautify him only lacks a cover.   88
The fish lives in the sea, and 'tis much pride   89
For fair without the fair within to hide.
That book in many's eyes doth share the glory,
That in gold clasps locks in the golden story;
So shall you share all that he doth possess,
By having him making yourself no less.

NURSE

No less? Nay, bigger! Women grow by men.   95

WIFE

Speak briefly, can you like of Paris' love?

JULIET

I'll look to like, if looking liking move;
But no more deep will I endart mine eye   98
Than your consent gives strength to make it fly.
        Enter Servingman.

SERVINGMAN Madam, the guests are come, supper
served up, you called, my young lady asked for, the
nurse cursed in the pantry, and everything in extremity. 102
I must hence to wait. I beseech you follow straight.

WIFE

We follow thee.   *[Exit Servingman.]*
        Juliet, the County stays.

NURSE

Go, girl, seek happy nights to happy days.   *Exeunt.*

*

---

85 *what . . . lies* i.e. his concealed inner qualities of character   86 *margent*
marginal gloss   88 *a cover* i.e. a wife   89–94 *The fish . . . no less* i.e. as the
sea enfolds the fish and the cover enfolds the book, so you shall enfold Paris
(in your arms), enhancing your good qualities by sharing his   95 *bigger*
i.e. through pregnancy   98 *endart mine eye* shoot my eye-glance (as an
arrow; cf. III, ii, 47)   102 *cursed in the pantry* i.e. the other servants
swear because the Nurse is not helping

I, iv   *Enter Romeo, Mercutio, Benvolio, with five or six*
               other Maskers; Torchbearers.

ROMEO

1   What, shall this speech be spoke for our excuse?
     Or shall we on without apology?

BENVOLIO

3   The date is out of such prolixity.
4   We'll have no Cupid hoodwinked with a scarf,
5   Bearing a Tartar's painted bow of lath,
6   Scaring the ladies like a crowkeeper;
7   [Nor no without-book prologue, faintly spoke
8   After the prompter, for our entrance;]
     But, let them measure us by what they will,
10   We'll measure them a measure and be gone.

ROMEO

     Give me a torch. I am not for this ambling.
12   Being but heavy, I will bear the light.

MERCUTIO

     Nay, gentle Romeo, we must have you dance.

ROMEO

     Not I, believe me. You have dancing shoes
     With nimble soles; I have a soul of lead
     So stakes me to the ground I cannot move.

MERCUTIO

     You are a lover. Borrow Cupid's wings
18   And soar with them above a common bound.

ROMEO

     I am too sore enpiercèd with his shaft
     To soar with his light feathers; and so bound

I, iv Before Capulet's house 1 *this speech* (Romeo has prepared a set
speech, such as customarily introduced visiting maskers) 3 *The date . .
prolixity* such superfluous speeches are now out of fashion 4 *hoodwinked*
blindfolded 5 *Tartar's . . . lath* (the Tartar's bow, used from horseback,
was much shorter than the English longbow) 6 *crowkeeper* scarecrow
7–8 (added from Q1) 7 *without-book* memorized 8 *entrance* (pronounced
'en-ter-ance' 10 *measure . . . measure* dance one dance 12 *heavy* sad, hence
'weighted down' 18 *bound* a leap, required in some dances

I cannot bound a pitch above dull woe.   21
Under love's heavy burden do I sink.

MERCUTIO
And, to sink in it, should you burden love –
Too great oppression for a tender thing.

ROMEO
Is love a tender thing? It is too rough,
Too rude, too boist'rous, and it pricks like thorn.

MERCUTIO
If love be rough with you, be rough with love,
Prick love for pricking, and you beat love down.
Give me a case to put my visage in.
A visor for a visor! What care I   30
What curious eye doth quote deformities?   31
Here are the beetle brows shall blush for me.   32

BENVOLIO
Come, knock and enter; and no sooner in
But every man betake him to his legs.   34

ROMEO
A torch for me! Let wantons light of heart
Tickle the senseless rushes with their heels;   ₁6
For I am proverbed with a grandsire phrase,   37
I'll be a candle-holder and look on;   38
The game was ne'er so fair, and I am done.   39

MERCUTIO
Tut! dun's the mouse, the constable's own word!   40
If thou art Dun, we'll draw thee from the mire   41

21 *pitch* height (falconry)   30 *A visor . . . visor* a mask for a face ugly enough to be itself a mask   31 *quote* note   32 *beetle brows* beetling eyebrows (of the mask)   34 *betake . . . legs* join the dance   36 *rushes* (used as floor coverings)   37 *grandsire phrase* old saying   38 *candle-holder* i.e. non-participant   39 *The game . . . done* best quit a game at the height of enjoyment (proverbial; cf. I, v, 119)   40 *dun's the mouse* be quiet as a mouse (proverbial); *constable's own word* i.e. the caution to be quiet   41 *Dun* (stock name for a horse); *mire* (alluding to a winter game, 'Dun is in the mire,' in which the players lifted a heavy log representing a horse caught in the mud)

42   Of this sir-reverence love, wherein thou stickest
43   Up to the ears. Come, we burn daylight, ho!

ROMEO
Nay, that's not so.

MERCUTIO   I mean, sir, in delay
We waste our lights in vain, like lamps by day.
Take our good meaning, for our judgments sits
47   Five times in that ere once in our five wits.

ROMEO
And we mean well in going to this masque,
49   But 'tis no wit to go.

MERCUTIO   Why, may one ask?

ROMEO
I dreamt a dream to-night.

MERCUTIO   And so did I.

ROMEO
Well, what was yours?

MERCUTIO   That dreamers often lie.

ROMEO
In bed asleep, while they do dream things true.

MERCUTIO
53   O, then I see Queen Mab hath been with you.
She is the fairies' midwife, and she comes
55   In shape no bigger than an agate stone
On the forefinger of an alderman,
57   Drawn with a team of little atomies
Over men's noses as they lie asleep;
59   Her wagon spokes made of long spinners' legs,
The cover, of the wings of grasshoppers;

42 *sir-reverence* filthy (literally 'save-your-reverence,' a euphemism associated with physical functions) 43 *burn daylight* waste time (proverbial) 47 *five wits* mental faculties: common sense (the perceptive power common to all five physical senses), fantasy, imagination, judgment (reason), memory 49 *no wit* not intelligent 53 *Mab* (a Celtic folk name for the fairy queen) 55 *agate stone* jewel carved with figures and set in a ring 57 *atomies* tiny creatures 59 *spinners* spiders

Her traces, of the smallest spider web ;   61
Her collars, of the moonshine's wat'ry beams ;   62
Her whip, of cricket's bone ; the lash, of film ;   63
Her wagoner, a small grey-coated gnat,
Not half so big as a round little worm   65
Pricked from the lazy finger of a maid ;
Her chariot is an empty hazelnut,
Made by the joiner squirrel or old grub,
Time out o' mind the fairies' coachmakers.
And in this state she gallops night by night
Through lovers' brains, and then they dream of love ;
O'er courtiers' knees, that dream on curtsies straight ;
O'er lawyers' fingers, who straight dream on fees ;
O'er ladies' lips, who straight on kisses dream,
Which oft the angry Mab with blisters plagues,
Because their breaths with sweetmeats tainted are.   76
Sometime she gallops o'er a courtier's nose,
And then dreams he of smelling out a suit ;   78
And sometime comes she with a tithe-pig's tail   79
Tickling a parson's nose as 'a lies asleep,
Then dreams he of another benefice.   81
Sometimes she driveth o'er a soldier's neck,
And then dreams he of cutting foreign throats,
Of breaches, ambuscadoes, Spanish blades,
Of healths five fathom deep ; and then anon   85
Drums in his ear, at which he starts and wakes,
And being thus frighted, swears a prayer or two
And sleeps again. This is that very Mab

61, 62 *traces, collars* parts of the harness   63 *film* any filament   65–66 *worm . . . maid* (alluding to the proverbial saying that worms breed in idle fingers)   76 *with sweetmeats* i.e. as a result of eating sweetmeats   78 *smelling . . . suit* discovering a petitioner who will pay for his influence with government officials   79 *tithe-pig* the parson's tithe (tenth) of his parishioner's livestock   81 *another benefice* an additional 'living' in the church   85 *healths . . . deep* drinking toasts from glasses thirty feet deep

That plats the manes of horses in the night
90 And bakes the elflocks in foul sluttish hairs,
Which once untangled much misfortune bodes.
92 This is the hag, when maids lie on their backs,
That presses them and learns them first to bear,
Making them women of good carriage.
This is she –
ROMEO   Peace, peace, Mercutio, peace!
96 Thou talk'st of nothing.
MERCUTIO   True, I talk of dreams;
Which are the children of an idle brain,
98 Begot of nothing but vain fantasy;
Which is as thin of substance as the air,
And more inconstant than the wind, who woos
Even now the frozen bosom of the North
And, being angered, puffs away from thence,
Turning his side to the dew-dropping South.
BENVOLIO
This wind you talk of blows us from ourselves.
Supper is done, and we shall come too late.
ROMEO
I fear, too early; for my mind misgives
107 Some consequence, yet hanging in the stars,
Shall bitterly begin his fearful date
With this night's revels and expire the term
Of a despisèd life, closed in my breast,
By some vile forfeit of untimely death.
112 But he that hath the steerage of my course
Direct my sail! On, lusty gentlemen!
BENVOLIO Strike, drum.

90 *elflocks* knots of tangled hair   92 *hag* night hag, or nightmare   96
nothing no tangible thing   98 *fantasy* (cf. l. 47 and note)   107 *consequence*
future chain of events; *hanging* (in astrology, future events are said to
'hang' – '*dependere*' – from the stars)   112 *he* God

They march about the stage, and Servingmen come **I, v**
forth with napkins.

1. SERVINGMAN Where's Potpan, that he helps not to 1
take away ? He shift a trencher ! he scrape a trencher ! 2

2. SERVINGMAN When good manners shall lie all in one 3
or two men's hands, and they unwashed too, 'tis a foul
thing.

1. SERVINGMAN Away with the joint-stools, remove the 6
court-cupboard, look to the plate. Good thou, save me 7
a piece of marchpane and, as thou loves me, let the 8
porter let in Susan Grindstone and Nell. *[Exit second* 9
Servingman.] Anthony, and Potpan !
[Enter two more Servingmen.]

3. SERVINGMAN Ay, boy, ready. 11

1. SERVINGMAN You are looked for and called for, asked
for and sought for, in the great chamber.

4. SERVINGMAN We cannot be here and there too. 14
Cheerly, boys ! Be brisk awhile, and the longer liver take 15
all. *[Exeunt third and fourth Servingmen.]*
Enter [Capulet, his Wife, Juliet, Tybalt, Nurse, and]
all the Guests and Gentlewomen to the Maskers.

CAPULET
Welcome, gentlemen ! Ladies that have their toes
Unplagued with corns will walk a bout with you. '7

I, v Within Capulet's house   s.d. (Q2 adds 'Enter Romeo,' altered in folio
to 'Enter Servant.' It is not certain that the Maskers leave the stage at
this point; 'marching about' itself sometimes signalled a change in locale.)
1, 3 *1. Servingman,* 2. *Servingman* (designated 'Servingman,' '1. Servingman' in Q2)   2 *trencher* wooden platter   3–5 *When . . . thing* (a complaint
that household decorum, 'good manners,' is sustained by too few, and
too untidy, servants)   6 *joint-stools* stools made by a joiner   7 *court-
cupboard* sideboard; *plate* silverware   8 *marchpane* sweetmeat with almonds
9 *Susan . . . Nell* (girls evidently invited for a servants' party in the kitchen
after the banquet)   11, 14 *3. Servingman,* 4. *Servingman* (designated '2.'
and '3.' in Q2, but presumably they are Anthony and Potpan, now arrived)
15 *longer . . . all* i.e. the spoils to the survivor (proverbial, but often used
in contexts like the above, advocating enjoyment of life)   17 *walk a bout*
dance a turn

Ah ha, my mistresses! which of you all
19 Will now deny to dance? She that makes dainty,
She I'll swear hath corns. Am I come near ye now?
Welcome, gentlemen! I have seen the day
That I have worn a visor and could tell
A whispering tale in a fair lady's ear,
Such as would please. 'Tis gone, 'tis gone, 'tis gone!
You are welcome, gentlemen! Come, musicians, play.
Music plays, and they dance.
26 A hall, a hall! give room! and foot it, girls.
More light, you knaves! and turn the tables up,
And quench the fire, the room is grown too hot.
29 Ah, sirrah, this unlooked-for sport comes well.
Nay, sit, nay, sit, good cousin Capulet,
For you and I are past our dancing days.
How long is't now since last yourself and I
Were in a mask?
33 2. CAPULET   By'r Lady, thirty years.
CAPULET
What, man? 'Tis not so much, 'tis not so much;
'Tis since the nuptial of Lucentio,
Come Pentecost as quickly as it will,
Some five-and-twenty years, and then we masked.
2. CAPULET
'Tis more, 'tis more. His son is elder, sir;
His son is thirty.
CAPULET   Will you tell me that?
40 His son was but a ward two years ago.
ROMEO *[to a Servingman]*
What lady's that, which doth enrich the hand
Of yonder knight?
SERVINGMAN   I know not, sir.

---

19 *makes dainty* pretends to hesitate   26 *A hall* clear the hall for dancing
29 *unlooked-for sport* (a dance was not originally planned)   33 *2. Capulet* (an
old man of the Capulet family); *thirty years* (indicating Capulet's advanced
age)   40 *His son . . . ago* it seems only two years since his son was a minor

ROMEO

O, she doth teach the torches to burn bright!
It seems she hangs upon the cheek of night
As a rich jewel in an Ethiop's ear –
Beauty too rich for use, for earth too dear!
So shows a snowy dove trooping with crows   48
As yonder lady o'er her fellows shows.
The measure done, I'll watch her place of stand
And, touching hers, make blessèd my rude hand.   51
Did my heart love till now? Forswear it, sight!
For I ne'er saw true beauty till this night.

TYBALT

This, by his voice, should be a Montague.
Fetch me my rapier, boy. What, dares the slave
Come hither, covered with an antic face,   56
To fleer and scorn at our solemnity?   57
Now, by the stock and honor of my kin,
To strike him dead I hold it not a sin.

CAPULET

Why, how now, kinsman? Wherefore storm you so?

TYBALT

Uncle, this is a Montague, our foe;
A villain, that is hither come in spite
To scorn at our solemnity this night.

CAPULET

Young Romeo is it?

TYBALT   'Tis he, that villain Romeo.

CAPULET

Content thee, gentle coz, let him alone.
'A bears him like a portly gentleman,   66
And, to say truth, Verona brags of him
To be a virtuous and well-governed youth.
I would not for the wealth of all this town
Here in my house do him disparagement.
Therefore be patient, take no note of him.

---

48 *with crows* (cf. I, ii, 89)   51 *rude* coarse-skinned   56 *antic face* comic
mask   57 *fleer* mock; *solemnity* dignified feast   66 *portly* of good carriage

It is my will, the which if thou respect,
Show a fair presence and put off these frowns,
An ill-beseeming semblance for a feast.

TYBALT

It fits when such a villain is a guest.
I'll not endure him.

CAPULET   He shall be endured.
What, goodman boy ! I say he shall. Go to !
Am I the master here, or you ? Go to !

79   You'll not endure him, God shall mend my soul !
80   You'll make a mutiny among my guests !
81   You will set cock-a-hoop, you'll be the man !

TYBALT

Why, uncle, 'tis a shame.

CAPULET   Go to, go to !
You are a saucy boy. Is't so, indeed ?

84   This trick may chance to scathe you. I know what.
85   You must contrary me ! Marry, 'tis time –
86   Well said, my hearts ! – You are a princox – go !
Be quiet, or – More light, more light ! – For shame !
I'll make you quiet ; what ! – Cheerly, my hearts !

TYBALT

89   Patience perforce with willful choler meeting
Makes my flesh tremble in their different greeting.
I will withdraw ; but this intrusion shall,
Now seeming sweet, convert to bitt'rest gall.   *Exit.*

ROMEO

93   If I profane with my unworthiest hand
94   This holy shrine, the gentle sin is this ;

---

79 *God . . . soul* (an expression of impatience)   80 *mutiny* violent disturbance   81 *set cock-a-hoop* i.e. take the lead; *be the man* play the big man   84 *scathe* injure; *what* what I'm doing   85 *'tis time* it's time you learned your place (?)   86 *said* done; *my hearts* (addressed to the dancers); *princox* saucy boy   89 *Patience perforce* enforced self-restraint; *choler* anger   93–110 (these lines form an English-style sonnet and the first quatrain of another)   94 *shrine* i.e. Juliet's hand; *sin* i.e. roughening her soft hand with his coarser one (cf. l. 51)

My lips, two blushing pilgrims, ready stand   95
  To smooth that rough touch with a tender kiss.

JULIET
Good pilgrim, you do wrong your hand too much,   97
  Which mannerly devotion shows in this ;
For saints have hands that pilgrims' hands do touch,
  And palm to palm is holy palmers' kiss.   100

ROMEO
Have not saints lips, and holy palmers too ?

JULIET
Ay, pilgrim, lips that they must use in prayer.

ROMEO
O, then, dear saint, let lips do what hands do !   103
  They pray ; grant thou, lest faith turn to despair.

JULIET
Saints do not move, though grant for prayers' sake.   105

ROMEO
Then move not while my prayer's effect I take.
Thus from my lips, by thine my sin is purged.
  [Kisses her.]

JULIET
Then have my lips the sin that they have took.

ROMEO
Sin from my lips ? O trespass sweetly urged !
  Give me my sin again.
  [Kisses her.]

JULIET   You kiss by th' book.   110

NURSE
Madam, your mother craves a word with you.

ROMEO
What is her mother ?

---

95 *pilgrims* (so called because pilgrims visit shrines)   **97–100** *Good . . . kiss*
your touch is not rough, to heal it with a kiss is unnecessary, a handclasp is
sufficient greeting   **100** *palmers* religious pilgrims   **103** *do what hands do*
i.e. press each other (in a kiss)   **105** *move* take the initiative; *grant* give
permission   **110** *book* book of etiquette

NURSE   Marry, bachelor,
   Her mother is the lady of the house,
   And a good lady, and a wise and virtuous.
115 I nursed her daughter that you talked withal.
   I tell you, he that can lay hold of her
117 Shall have the chinks.
NURSE   Is she a Capulet?

ROMEO   Is she a Capulet?
118 O dear account! my life is my foe's debt.

BENVOLIO
119 Away, be gone; the sport is at the best.

ROMEO
   Ay, so I fear; the more is my unrest.

CAPULET
   Nay, gentlemen, prepare not to be gone;
122 We have a trifling foolish banquet towards.
   Is it e'en so? Why then, I thank you all.
   I thank you, honest gentlemen. Good night.
   More torches here! Come on then, let's to bed.
126 Ah, sirrah, by my fay, it waxes late;
   I'll to my rest.   *[Exeunt all but Juliet and Nurse.]*

JULIET
   Come hither, nurse. What is yond gentleman?

NURSE
   The son and heir of old Tiberio.

JULIET
   What's he that now is going out of door?

NURSE
   Marry, that, I think, be young Petruchio.

JULIET
   What's he that follows there, that would not dance?

NURSE
   I know not.

JULIET
   Go ask his name. – If he be marrièd,

---

115 *withal* with   117 *chinks* money   118 *my foe's debt* owed to my foe   119 *Away . . . best* (cf. I, iv, 39)   122 *banquet* light refreshments; *towards* in preparation   126 *fay* faith

My grave is like to be my wedding bed.

NURSE

His name is Romeo, and a Montague,
The only son of your great enemy.

JULIET

My only love, sprung from my only hate!
Too early seen unknown, and known too late!
Prodigious birth of love it is to me   140
That I must love a loathèd enemy.

NURSE

What's tis? what's tis?   142

JULIET   A rhyme I learnt even now
Of one I danced withal.
        One calls within, 'Juliet.'

NURSE   Anon, anon!   143
Come, let's away; the strangers all are gone.   *Exeunt.*

*

        [Enter] Chorus.   II, Cho

CHORUS

Now old desire doth in his deathbed lie,   1
    And young affection gapes to be his heir;   2
That fair for which love groaned for and would die,
    With tender Juliet matched, is now not fair.
Now Romeo is beloved and loves again,
    Alike bewitchèd by the charm of looks;
But to his foe supposed he must complain,   7
    And she steal love's sweet bait from fearful hooks.   8
Being held a foe, he may not have access
    To breathe such vows as lovers use to swear,   10

140 *Prodigious* monstrous   142 *tis* this   143 *Anon* i.e. we are coming right
away
II, Cho.   1 *old desire* i.e. Romeo's love of Rosaline   2 *young affection* new
love; *gapes* opens his mouth hungrily   7 *complain* make a lover's plaints
8 *steal . . . hooks* (a popular conceit: the lover 'fishes' for his beloved. For
Juliet to be 'caught' is dangerous because of the family feud.)   10 *use* are
accustomed

And she as much in love, her means much less
　　To meet her new belovèd anywhere;
But passion lends them power, time means, to meet,
Temp'ring extremities with extreme sweet.   *[Exit.]*

II, i   *Enter Romeo alone.*

ROMEO

1　Can I go forward when my heart is here?
2　Turn back, dull earth, and find thy centre out.
　　Enter Benvolio with Mercutio. [Romeo retires.]

BENVOLIO

Romeo! my cousin Romeo! Romeo!

MERCUTIO   He is wise,
And, on my life, hath stol'n him home to bed.

BENVOLIO

He ran this way and leapt this orchard wall.
Call, good Mercutio.

6 MERCUTIO   Nay, I'll conjure too.
7　Romeo! humors! madman! passion! lover!
　Appear thou in the likeness of a sigh;
　Speak but one rhyme, and I am satisfied!
　Cry but 'Ay me!' pronounce but 'love' and 'dove';
11　Speak to my gossip Venus one fair word,
12　One nickname for her purblind son and heir
13　Young Abraham Cupid, he that shot so true
14　When King Cophetua loved the beggar maid!
　He heareth not, he stirreth not, he moveth not;
16　The ape is dead, and I must conjure him.

II, i Within Capulet's walled orchard　1 *my heart is here* (the Neo-Platonic fancy that the heart or soul of the lover dwells in the beloved)　2 *earth* i.e. my body; *centre* i.e. my heart or soul　6 *Nay . . too* (printed as part of preceding speech in Q2)　7 *humors* whims　11 *gossip* female crony 12 *purblind* dim-sighted　13 *Young Abraham* youthful, yet patriarchal (Cupid, or Love, was both the youngest and the oldest of the gods)　14 *King Cophetua . . . beggar maid* (from a popular ballad)　16 *The ape . . . him* (probably recalling a showman's ape who 'played dead' until called with the right word-formula)

I conjure thee by Rosaline's bright eyes,
By her high forehead and her scarlet lip,
By her fine foot, straight leg, and quivering thigh,
And the demesnes that there adjacent lie,   20
That in thy likeness thou appear to us!

BENVOLIO
An if he hear thee, thou wilt anger him.

MERCUTIO
This cannot anger him. 'Twould anger him
To raise a spirit in his mistress' circle   24
Of some strange nature, letting it there stand
Till she had laid it and conjured it down.
That were some spite; my invocation
Is fair and honest: in his mistress' name,
I conjure only but to raise up him.

BENVOLIO
Come, he hath hid himself among these trees
To be consorted with the humorous night.   31
Blind is his love and best befits the dark.

MERCUTIO
If love be blind, love cannot hit the mark.
Now will he sit under a medlar tree
And wish his mistress were that kind of fruit
As maids call medlars when they laugh alone.   36
O, Romeo, that she were, O that she were
An open et cetera, thou a pop'rin pear!   38
Romeo, good night. I'll to my truckle-bed;   39
This field-bed is too cold for me to sleep.
Come, shall we go?

BENVOLIO   Go then, for 'tis in vain
To seek him here that means not to be found.
Exit [with Mercutio].

20 *demesnes* domains 24 *circle* the conjurer's circle in which an evoked
spirit supposedly appears (Mercutio intends a ribald pun) 31 *humorous*
damp; also, capricious 36, 38 *medlars, pop'rin pear* fruits (used vulgarly
in reference to the sex organs) 39 *truckle-bed* trundle bed

II, ii ROMEO *[coming forward]*

He jests at scars that never felt a wound.
[Enter Juliet above at a window.]
But soft! What light through yonder window breaks?
It is the East, and Juliet is the sun!
4   Arise, fair sun, and kill the envious moon,
Who is already sick and pale with grief
6   That thou her maid art far more fair than she.
Be not her maid, since she is envious.
8   Her vestal livery is but sick and green,
And none but fools do wear it. Cast it off.
It is my lady; O, it is my love!
O that she knew she were!
She speaks, yet she says nothing. What of that?
Her eye discourses; I will answer it.
I am too bold; 'tis not to me she speaks.
Two of the fairest stars in all the heaven,
Having some business, do entreat her eyes
17   To twinkle in their spheres till they return.
What if her eyes were there, they in her head?
The brightness of her cheek would shame those stars
As daylight doth a lamp; her eyes in heaven
Would through the airy region stream so bright
That birds would sing and think it were not night.
See how she leans her cheek upon her hand!
O that I were a glove upon that hand,
That I might touch that cheek!

JULIET   Ay me!

ROMEO   She speaks.

O, speak again, bright angel! for thou art
As glorious to this night, being o'er my head,
As is a wingèd messenger of heaven

II, ii   **4** *kill* make invisible by more intense light   **6** *her maid* (Diana, moon-goddess, was patroness of virgins)   **8** *vestal livery* virginity (after Vesta, another virgin goddess); *green* anemic   **17** *spheres* orbits

Unto the white-upturnèd wond'ring eyes   29
Of mortals that fall back to gaze on him
When he bestrides the lazy-pacing clouds
And sails upon the bosom of the air.

JULIET
O Romeo, Romeo! wherefore art thou Romeo?
Deny thy father and refuse thy name;
Or, if thou wilt not, be but sworn my love,
And I'll no longer be a Capulet.

ROMEO [aside]
Shall I hear more, or shall I speak at this?

JULIET
'Tis but thy name that is my enemy.
Thou art thyself, though not a Montague.
What's Montague? It is nor hand, nor foot,
Nor arm, nor face, nor any other part
Belonging to a man. O, be some other name!
What's in a name? That which we call a rose
By any other name would smell as sweet.   44
So Romeo would, were he not Romeo called,
Retain that dear perfection which he owes   46
Without that title. Romeo, doff thy name;
And for thy name, which is no part of thee,
Take all myself.

ROMEO   I take thee at thy word.
Call me but love, and I'll be new baptized;
Henceforth I never will be Romeo.

JULIET
What man art thou that, thus bescreened in night,
So stumblest on my counsel?

ROMEO   By a name
I know not how to tell thee who I am.
My name, dear saint, is hateful to myself,
Because it is an enemy to thee.

---

29 *white-upturnèd* (the whites show when the eyes are turned upward)
44 *name* (from Q1; Q2 reads 'word,' perhaps correctly)   46 *owes* owns

Had I it written, I would tear the word.

JULIET
My ears have yet not drunk a hundred words
Of thy tongue's uttering, yet I know the sound.
Art thou not Romeo, and a Montague?

ROMEO
61   Neither, fair maid, if either thee dislike.

JULIET
How camest thou hither, tell me, and wherefore?
The orchard walls are high and hard to climb,
And the place death, considering who thou art,
If any of my kinsmen find thee here.

ROMEO
66   With love's light wings did I o'erperch these walls;
For stony limits cannot hold love out,
And what love can do, that dares love attempt.
Therefore thy kinsmen are no stop to me.

JULIET
If they do see thee, they will murder thee.

ROMEO
Alack, there lies more peril in thine eye
Than twenty of their swords! Look thou but sweet,
73   And I am proof against their enmity.

JULIET
I would not for the world they saw thee here.

ROMEO
I have night's cloak to hide me from their eyes;
And but thou love me, let them find me here.
My life were better ended by their hate
78   Than death proroguèd, wanting of thy love.

JULIET
By whose direction found'st thou out this place?

ROMEO
By love, that first did prompt me to inquire.

---

61 *dislike* displease   **66** *o'erperch* fly over   **73** *proof* armored   **78** *pro-roguèd* postponed; *wanting of* lacking

He lent me counsel, and I lent him eyes.
I am no pilot; yet, wert thou as far
As that vast shore washed with the farthest sea,   83
I should adventure for such merchandise.   84

JULIET
Thou knowest the mask of night is on my face;
Else would a maiden blush bepaint my cheek
For that which thou hast heard me speak to-night.
Fain would I dwell on form – fain, fain deny
What I have spoke; but farewell compliment!   89
Dost thou love me? I know thou wilt say 'Ay';
And I will take thy word. Yet, if thou swear'st,
Thou mayst prove false. At lovers' perjuries,
They say Jove laughs. O gentle Romeo,
If thou dost love, pronounce it faithfully.
Or if thou thinkest I am too quickly won,
I'll frown, and be perverse, and say thee nay,
So thou wilt woo; but else, not for the world.
In truth, fair Montague, I am too fond,
And therefore thou mayst think my havior light;   99
But trust me, gentleman, I'll prove more true
Than those that have more cunning to be strange.   101
I should have been more strange, I must confess,
But that thou overheard'st, ere I was ware,   103
My true-love passion. Therefore pardon me,
And not impute this yielding to light love,
Which the dark night hath so discoverèd.   106

ROMEO
Lady, by yonder blessèd moon I vow,
That tips with silver all these fruit-tree tops –

JULIET
O, swear not by the moon, th' inconstant moon,
That monthly changes in her circled orb,

83 *farthest sea* the Pacific 84 *adventure* risk a voyage 89 *compliment*
etiquette 99 *havior* behavior 101 *strange* aloof, distant 103 *ware* aware
of you 106 *discoverèd* revealed

    Lest that thy love prove likewise variable.

ROMEO

    What shall I swear by?

JULIET   Do not swear at all;
    Or if thou wilt, swear by thy gracious self,
    Which is the god of my idolatry,
    And I'll believe thee.

ROMEO   If my heart's dear love—

JULIET

    Well, do not swear. Although I joy in thee,
    I have no joy of this contract to-night.
    It is too rash, too unadvised, too sudden;
    Too like the lightning, which doth cease to be
120   Ere one can say 'It lightens.' Sweet, good night!
    This bud of love, by summer's ripening breath,
    May prove a beauteous flow'r when next we meet.
    Good night, good night! As sweet repose and rest
    Come to thy heart as that within my breast!

ROMEO

    O, wilt thou leave me so unsatisfied?

JULIET

    What satisfaction canst thou have to-night?

ROMEO

    Th' exchange of thy love's faithful vow for mine.

JULIET

    I gave thee mine before thou didst request it;
    And yet I would it were to give again.

ROMEO

    Wouldst thou withdraw it? For what purpose, love?

JULIET

131   But to be frank and give it thee again.
    And yet I wish but for the thing I have.
133   My bounty is as boundless as the sea,
    My love as deep; the more I give to thee,

131 *frank* generous   133 *bounty* wish to give (love)

The more I have, for both are infinite.   135
I hear some noise within. Dear love, adieu !
    [Nurse calls within.]
Anon, good nurse ! Sweet Montague, be true.
Stay but a little, I will come again.   *[Exit.]*

ROMEO

O blessèd, blessèd night ! I am afeard,
Being in night, all this is but a dream,
Too flattering-sweet to be substantial.
    [Enter Juliet above.]

JULIET

Three words, dear Romeo, and good night indeed.
If that thy bent of love be honorable,   143
Thy purpose marriage, send me word to-morrow,
By one that I'll procure to come to thee,
Where and what time thou wilt perform the rite ;
And all my fortunes at thy foot I'll lay
And follow thee my lord throughout the world.

NURSE *[within]* Madam !

JULIET

I come, anon. – But if thou meanest not well,
I do beseech thee –

NURSE *[within]*
Madam !

JULIET   By and by I come. –   152
To cease thy suit and leave me to my grief.
To-morrow will I send.

ROMEO   So thrive my soul –

JULIET

A thousand times good night !   *[Exit.]*

ROMEO

A thousand times the worse, to want thy light !
Love goes toward love as schoolboys from their books ;

---

135 *The more I have* (scholastic theologians debated how love could be
given away and yet the giver have more than before; cf. Dante, *Purgatorio*.
XV 61 ff.)   **143** *bent* purpose   **152** *By and by* immediately

But love from love, toward school with heavy looks.
Enter Juliet [above] again.

JULIET
Hist! Romeo, hist! O for a falc'ner's voice

160 To lure this tassel-gentle back again!

161 Bondage is hoarse and may not speak aloud,
Else would I tear the cave where Echo lies
And make her airy tongue more hoarse than mine
With repetition of 'My Romeo!'

ROMEO
165 It is my soul that calls upon my name.
How silver-sweet sound lovers' tongues by night,

167 Like softest music to attending ears!

JULIET
Romeo!

ROMEO   My sweet?

JULIET   At what o'clock to-morrow
Shall I send to thee?

ROMEO   By the hour of nine.

JULIET
I will not fail. 'Tis twenty years till then.
I have forgot why I did call thee back.

ROMEO
Let me stand here till thou remember it.

JULIET
I shall forget, to have thee still stand there,
Rememb'ring how I love thy company.

ROMEO
And I'll still stay, to have thee still forget,
Forgetting any other home but this.

JULIET
'Tis almost morning. I would have thee gone —

178 And yet no farther than a wanton's bird,

---

160 *tassel-gentle* tercel-gentle, or male falcon   **161** *Bondage* (she feels 'imprisoned' by the nearness of her kinsmen)   **165** *my soul* (cf. II, i, 1 and note)   **167** *attending* paying attention   **178** *wanton* spoiled child

That lets it hop a little from her hand,
Like a poor prisoner in his twisted gyves,   180
And with a silken thread plucks it back again,
So loving-jealous of his liberty.

ROMEO
I would I were thy bird.

JULIET   Sweet, so would I.
Yet I should kill thee with much cherishing.   184
Good night, good night! Parting is such sweet sorrow
That I shall say good night till it be morrow.   *[Exit.]* 186

ROMEO
Sleep dwell upon thine eyes, peace in thy breast!   187
Would I were sleep and peace, so sweet to rest!
Hence will I to my ghostly father's cell,   189
His help to crave and my dear hap to tell.   *Exit.*   190

*

Enter Friar [Laurence] alone, with a basket.   II, iii

FRIAR
The grey-eyed morn smiles on the frowning night,
Check'ring the Eastern clouds with streaks of light;
And fleckèd darkness like a drunkard reels   3
From forth day's path and Titan's fiery wheels.   4
Now, ere the sun advance his burning eye
The day to cheer and night's dank dew to dry,
I must up-fill this osier cage of ours   7
With baleful weeds and precious-juicèd flowers.

---

180 *gyves* fetters   **184** *cherishing* caressing   **186** *morrow* morning   **187–90** (In Q2 the speech-prefix 'Juliet' is mistakenly placed before the first of these lines, and they are followed by four lines that are nearly identical with those at II, iii, 1–4. Perhaps Shakespeare decided to let the Friar announce the dawn instead of Romeo, and the cancelled lines in the manuscript were printed in error.)   **189** *ghostly* spiritual   **190** *dear hap* good luck
II, iii Before Friar Laurence's cell   **3** *fleckèd* spotted, dappled   **4** *Titan's fiery wheels* the sun's chariot wheels   **7** *osier cage* willow basket

The earth that's nature's mother is her tomb.
What is her burying grave, that is her womb;
And from her womb children of divers kind
We sucking on her natural bosom find,
Many for many virtues excellent,
None but for some, and yet all different.
15 O, mickle is the powerful grace that lies
In plants, herbs, stones, and their true qualities;
For naught so vile that on the earth doth live
But to the earth some special good doth give;
Nor aught so good but, strained from that fair use,
20 Revolts from true birth, stumbling on abuse.
Virtue itself turns vice, being misapplied,
22 And vice sometime's by action dignified.
            Enter Romeo.
Within the infant rind of this weak flower
Poison hath residence, and medicine power;
25 For this, being smelt, with that part cheers each part;
Being tasted, slays all senses with the heart.
27 Two such opposèd kings encamp them still
28 In man as well as herbs – grace and rude will;
And where the worser is predominant,
30 Full soon the canker death eats up that plant.

ROMEO
31 Good morrow, father.

FRIAR   Benedicite!
What early tongue so sweet saluteth me?
Young son, it argues a distemperèd head
So soon to bid good morrow to thy bed.
Care keeps his watch in every old man's eye,
And where care lodges, sleep will never lie;

---

15 *mickle* much   20 *true birth* its true nature   22 *dignified* made worthy;
s.d. (this entrance seems premature, but cf. entrance of Nurse at III, iii, 70)
25–26 *being . . . heart* i.e. being smelt, stimulates; being tasted, kills   27 *still*
always   28 *grace* power of goodness; *rude will* coarse impulses of the flesh
30 *canker* the worm in the bud   31 *morrow* morning; *Benedicite* bless you

But where unbruisèd youth with unstuffed brain 37
Doth couch his limbs, there golden sleep doth reign.
Therefore thy earliness doth me assure
Thou art uproused with some distemp'rature;
Or if not so, then here I hit it right –
Our Romeo hath not been in bed to-night.

ROMEO
That last is true – the sweeter rest was mine.

FRIAR
God pardon sin! Wast thou with Rosaline?

ROMEO
With Rosaline, my ghostly father? No.
I have forgot that name and that name's woe.

FRIAR
That's my good son! But where hast thou been then?

ROMEO
I'll tell thee ere thou ask it me again.
I have been feasting with mine enemy,
Where on a sudden one hath wounded me
That's by me wounded. Both our remedies
Within thy help and holy physic lies. 52
I bear no hatred, blessèd man, for, lo,
My intercession likewise steads my foe. 54

FRIAR
Be plain, good son, and homely in thy drift. 55
Riddling confession finds but riddling shrift. 56

ROMEO
Then plainly know my heart's dear love is set
On the fair daughter of rich Capulet;
As mine on hers, so hers is set on mine,
And all combined, save what thou must combine
By holy marriage. When, and where, and how
We met, we wooed, and made exchange of vow,
I'll tell thee as we pass; but this I pray,

---

37 *unstuffed* carefree 52 *physic* medicine 54 *intercession* request; *steads*
benefits 55 *homely* simple; *drift* explanation 56 *shrift* absolution

That thou consent to marry us to-day.

FRIAR

Holy Saint Francis ! What a change is here !
Is Rosaline, that thou didst love so dear,
So soon forsaken ? Young men's love then lies
Not truly in their hearts, but in their eyes.
Jesu Maria ! What a deal of brine
Hath washed thy sallow cheeks for Rosaline !
How much salt water thrown away in waste
72 To season love, that of it doth not taste !
The sun not yet thy sighs from heaven clears,
Thy old groans ring yet in mine ancient ears.
Lo, here upon thy cheek the stain doth sit
Of an old tear that is not washed off yet.
If e'er thou wast thyself, and these woes thine,
Thou and these woes were all for Rosaline.
And art thou changed ? Pronounce this sentence then :
80 Women may fall when there's no strength in men.

ROMEO

Thou chid'st me oft for loving Rosaline.

FRIAR

For doting, not for loving, pupil mine.

ROMEO

And bad'st me bury love.

FRIAR   Not in a grave
To lay one in, another out to have.

ROMEO

I pray thee chide not. She whom I love now
86 Doth grace for grace and love for love allow.
The other did not so.

FRIAR   O, she knew well
88 Thy love did read by rote, that could not spell.
But come, young waverer, come go with me.

---

72 *season* flavor; *doth not taste* i.e. now has no savor   **80** *strength* constancy
86 *grace* favor   **88** *by rote . . . spell* like a child repeating words without
understanding them

In one respect I'll thy assistant be;
For this alliance may so happy prove
To turn your households' rancor to pure love.

ROMEO
O, let us hence! I stand on sudden haste. 93

FRIAR
Wisely and slow. They stumble that run fast. *Exeunt*.

*

Enter Benvolio and Mercutio. II, iv

MERCUTIO
Where the devil should this Romeo be?
Came he not home to-night?

BENVOLIO
Not to his father's. I spoke with his man.

MERCUTIO
Why, that same pale hard-hearted wench, that Rosaline,
Torments him so that he will sure run mad.

BENVOLIO
Tybalt, the kinsman to old Capulet,
Hath sent a letter to his father's house.

MERCUTIO A challenge, on my life.

BENVOLIO Romeo will answer it.

MERCUTIO Any man that can write may answer a letter. 10

BENVOLIO Nay, he will answer the letter's master, how
he dares, being dared.

MERCUTIO Alas, poor Romeo, he is already dead!
stabbed with a white wench's black eye; run through the
ear with a love song; the very pin of his heart cleft with 15
the blind bow-boy's butt-shaft; and is he a man to en- 16
counter Tybalt?

93 *on* in need of
II, iv A street in Verona   10 *answer* accept   15 *pin* peg in the centre of
a target, bull's eye   16 *bow-boy's butt-shaft* Cupid's arrow (jestingly
identified as a barbless target-arrow)   16–17 *is . . . Tybalt* (Mercutio has
doubts of Romeo's prowess while he is despondent and low-spirited)

BENVOLIO Why, what is Tybalt?

19 MERCUTIO More than Prince of Cats, I can tell you. O,
20 he's the courageous captain of compliments. He fights as
21 you sing pricksong – keeps time, distance, and propor-
22 tion; he rests his minim rests, one, two, and the third in
23 your bosom! the very butcher of a silk button, a duellist,
24 a duellist! a gentleman of the very first house, of the first
25 and second cause. Ah, the immortal passado! the punto
26 reverso! the hay!

BENVOLIO The what?

28 MERCUTIO The pox of such antic, lisping, affecting fantasticoes – these new tuners of accent! 'By Jesu, a very
30 good blade! a very tall man! a very good whore!' Why,
31 is not this a lamentable thing, grandsir, that we should be
thus afflicted with these strange flies, these fashion-
33 mongers, these pardon-me's, who stand so much on the
34 new form that they cannot sit at ease on the old bench?
35 O, their bones, their bones!

Enter Romeo.

BENVOLIO Here comes Romeo! here comes Romeo!

37 MERCUTIO Without his roe, like a dried herring. O flesh,
38 flesh, how art thou fishified! Now is he for the numbers
39 that Petrarch flowed in. Laura, to his lady, was a
kitchen wench (marry, she had a better love to berhyme
41 her), Dido a dowdy, Cleopatra a gypsy, Helen and Hero

---

19 *Prince of Cats* (Tybalt, or Tybert, is the cat's name in medieval stories of Reynard the Fox) **20** *compliments* etiquette **21** *pricksong* written music **22** *minim rests* shortest rests (in the old musical notation); *third* third rapier thrust **23** *button* i.e. on his opponent's shirt **24** *first house* finest fencing school **24–25** *first and second cause* causes for a challenge (in the duellist's code) **25** *passado* lunge **25–26** *punto reverso* backhanded stroke **26** *hay* home-thrust (from '*hai*,' 'I have it'; a new term to Benvolio) **28** *fantasticoes* coxcombs **30** *tall* brave **31** *grandsir* good sir **33** *pardon-me's* i.e. sticklers for etiquette **34** *form* (1) fashion, (2) schoolbench; *old bench* i.e. native manners and learning **35** *bones* Fr. 'good's': '*bon's*' **37** *Without his roe* i.e. 'shot' **38** *numbers* verses **39** *Laura* Petrarch's beloved; *to* in comparison with **41** *Dido* Queen of Carthage who fell in love with Aeneas; *Helen* Helen of Troy; *Hero* beloved of Leander

hildings and harlots, Thisbe a grey eye or so, but not to 42
the purpose. Signior Romeo, bon jour! There's a French 43
salutation to your French slop. You gave us the counter- 44
feit fairly last night. 45

ROMEO Good morrow to you both. What counterfeit did
I give you?

MERCUTIO The slip, sir, the slip. Can you not conceive? 48

ROMEO Pardon, good Mercutio. My business was great,
and in such a case as mine a man may strain courtesy.

MERCUTIO That's as much as to say, such a case as yours 51
constrains a man to bow in the hams. 52

ROMEO Meaning, to curtsy.

MERCUTIO Thou hast most kindly hit it. 54

ROMEO A most courteous exposition.

MERCUTIO Nay, I am the very pink of courtesy.

ROMEO Pink for flower. 57

MERCUTIO Right.

ROMEO Why, then is my pump well-flowered. 59

MERCUTIO Sure wit, follow me this jest now till thou
hast worn out thy pump, that, when the single sole of it
is worn, the jest may remain, after the wearing, solely 62
singular.

ROMEO O single-soled jest, solely singular for the single- 64
ness!

MERCUTIO Come between us, good Benvolio! My wits 66
faint.

ROMEO Swits and spurs, swits and spurs! or I'll cry a 67
match.

42 *hildings* worthless creatures; *Thisbe* (Pyramus and Thisbe were young lovers whose story resembles that of Romeo and Juliet) 42–43 *not to the purpose* not worth mentioning 43 *bon jour* good day 44 *slop* trousers 45 *fairly* effectively 48 *slip* (1) escape, (2) counterfeit coin 51 *such . . . yours* the pox (implied) 52 *hams* hips 54 *kindly hit it* interpreted it in your own way 57 *flower* ('flower of courtesy' was the usual complimentary form; cf. II, v, 43) 59 *pump* shoe; *well-flowered* (because pinked, or punched, with an ornamental design) 62–63 *solely singular* uniquely remarkable 64 *single-soled* weak; *singleness* weakness 66 *My wits faint* my mind fails in this intricate word play 67 *Swits and spurs* switches and spurs, i.e. keep your horse (wit) running; *cry a match* claim victory

68 MERCUTIO Nay, if our wits run the wild-goose chase, I
am done; for thou hast more of the wild goose in one of
70 thy wits than, I am sure, I have in my whole five. Was I
with you there for the goose?

72 ROMEO Thou wast never with me for anything when
thou wast not there for the goose.

MERCUTIO I will bite thee by the ear for that jest.

75 ROMEO Nay, good goose, bite not!

76 MERCUTIO Thy wit is a very bitter sweeting; it is a most
sharp sauce.

78 ROMEO And is it not, then, well served in to a sweet goose?

79 MERCUTIO O, here's a wit of cheveril, that stretches from
80 an inch narrow to an ell broad!

ROMEO I stretch it out for that word 'broad,' which, added
82 to the goose, proves thee far and wide a broad goose.

MERCUTIO Why, is not this better now than groaning for
love? Now art thou sociable, now art thou Romeo; now
art thou what thou art, by art as well as by nature. For
86 this drivelling love is like a great natural that runs lolling
87 up and down to hide his bauble in a hole.

BENVOLIO Stop there, stop there!

89 MERCUTIO Thou desirest me to stop in my tale against
the hair.

91 BENVOLIO Thou wouldst else have made thy tale large.

MERCUTIO O, thou art deceived! I would have made it
short; for I was come to the whole depth of my tale, and
94 meant indeed to occupy the argument no longer.

---

68 *wild-goose chase* cross-country horse race of 'follow the leader'   70–71
Was . . . goose was I accurate in calling you a goose   72–73 *Thou . . . goose*
you were never in my company for any purpose when you weren't looking
for a prostitute (goose)   75 *good . . . not* spare me (proverbial)   76 *bitter
sweeting* a tart species of apple   78 *sweet* tasty, tender   79 *cheveril* kid-skin,
easily stretched   80 *ell* forty-five inches (English measure)   82 *broad
goose* possibly, a goose from the Broads, shallow Norfolk lakes (?)   86
natural idiot   87 *bauble* jester's wand, here a phallic symbol   89–90
against the hair with my hair rubbed the wrong way, against my inclination
91 *large* broad, indecent   94 *occupy the argument* pursue the subject

ROMEO Here's goodly gear!   95
    Enter Nurse and her Man [Peter].

MERCUTIO A sail, a sail!

BENVOLIO Two, two! a shirt and a smock.   97

NURSE Peter!

PETER Anon.

NURSE My fan, Peter.

MERCUTIO Good Peter, to hide her face; for her fan 's
    the fairer face.

NURSE God ye good morrow, gentlemen.

MERCUTIO God ye good-den, fair gentlewoman.

NURSE Is it good-den?   105

MERCUTIO 'Tis no less, I tell ye; for the bawdy hand of
    the dial is now upon the prick of noon.   107

NURSE Out upon you! What a man are you!

ROMEO One, gentlewoman, that God hath made for him-
    self to mar.

NURSE By my troth, it is well said. 'For himself to mar,'
    quoth 'a? Gentlemen, can any of you tell me where I   112
    may find the young Romeo?

ROMEO I can tell you; but young Romeo will be older
    when you have found him than he was when you sought
    him. I am the youngest of that name, for fault of a worse.   116

NURSE You say well.

MERCUTIO Yea, is the worst well? Very well took, i'   118
    faith! wisely, wisely.

NURSE If you be he, sir, I desire some confidence with you.   120

BENVOLIO She will endite him to some supper.   121

MERCUTIO A bawd, a bawd, a bawd! So ho!   122

ROMEO What hast thou found?

---

95 *gear* stuff   97 *shirt, smock* male and female garments   105 *Is it good-den*
is it already afternoon   107 *prick* (1) indented point on a clock-face or
sundial, (2) phallus   112 *quoth 'a* said he   116 *for . . . worse* (parodying 'for
want of a better')   118 *took* understood   120 *confidence* conference
(malapropism)   121 *endite* invite (anticipating a malapropism)   122 *So ho*
(hunter's cry on sighting game)

124 MERCUTIO No hare, sir ; unless a hare, sir, in a lenten pie,
125   that is something stale and hoar ere it be spent.
          [He walks by them and sings.]
                An old hare hoar,
                And an old hare hoar,
             Is very good meat in Lent ;
               But a hare that is hoar
               Is too much for a score
           When it hoars ere it be spent.
    Romeo, will you come to your father's ? We'll to dinner
    thither.
    ROMEO I will follow you.
135 MERCUTIO Farewell, ancient lady. Farewell, *[sings]* lady,
    lady, lady.   *Exeunt [Mercutio, Benvolio].*
    NURSE I pray you, sir, what saucy merchant was this that
138   was so full of his ropery ?
    ROMEO A gentleman, nurse, that loves to hear himself
    talk and will speak more in a minute than he will stand
    to in a month.
    NURSE An 'a speak anything against me, I'll take him
    down, an 'a were lustier than he is, and twenty such
    Jacks ; and if I cannot, I'll find those that shall. Scurvy
145   knave ! I am none of his flirt-gills ; I am none of his
146   skains-mates. And thou must stand by too, and suffer
    every knave to use me at his pleasure !
148 PETER I saw no man use you at his pleasure. If I had, my
    weapon should quickly have been out, I warrant you. I
    dare draw as soon as another man, if I see occasion in a
    good quarrel, and the law on my side.
    NURSE Now, afore God, I am so vexed that every part
    about me quivers. Scurvy knave ! Pray you, sir, a word ;
    and, as I told you, my young lady bid me inquire you

---

124 *hare* i.e. prostitute; *lenten pie* meat pie eaten sparingly during Lent
125 *hoar* (1) grey with mould, (2) grey-haired, with wordplay on 'whore';
s.d. (from Q1) 135–36 *lady, lady, lady* (ballad refrain from *Chaste Susanna*)
138 *ropery* vulgar jesting 145 *flirt-gills* flirting Jills 146 *skains-mates*
outlaws, gangster molls 148–49 *my weapon . . . out* (cf. I, i, 30 and n.)

out. What she bid me say, I will keep to myself; but
first let me tell ye, if ye should lead her into a fool's 156
paradise, as they say, it were a very gross kind of behavior, as they say; for the gentlewoman is young; and
therefore, if you should deal double with her, truly it
were an ill thing to be offered to any gentlewoman, and
very weak dealing.   161

ROMEO Nurse, commend me to thy lady and mistress. I
protest unto thee –

NURSE Good heart, and i' faith I will tell her as much.
Lord, Lord! she will be a joyful woman.

ROMEO What wilt thou tell her, nurse? Thou dost not
mark me.

NURSE I will tell her, sir, that you do protest, which, as I
take it, is a gentlemanlike offer.

ROMEO
Bid her devise
Some means to come to shrift this afternoon;
And there she shall at Friar Laurence' cell
Be shrived and married. Here is for thy pains.

NURSE No, truly, sir; not a penny.

ROMEO Go to! I say you shall.

NURSE This afternoon, sir? Well, she shall be there.

ROMEO
And stay, good nurse, behind the abbey wall.
Within this hour my man shall be with thee
And bring thee cords made like a tackled stair,   178
Which to the high topgallant of my joy   179
Must be my convoy in the secret night.   180
Farewell. Be trusty, and I'll quit thy pains.   181
Farewell. Commend me to thy mistress.

NURSE
Now God in heaven bless thee! Hark you, sir.

156–57 *lead   . paradise* seduce her (proverbial) 161 *weak* unmanly
178 *tackled stair* rope ladder 179 *topgallant* mast and sail above the
mainmast 180 *convoy* conveyance 181 *quit thy pains* reward your efforts

ROMEO
> What say'st thou, my dear nurse?

NURSE
> Is your man secret? Did you ne'er hear say,
> Two may keep counsel, putting one away?

ROMEO
> I warrant thee my man's as true as steel.

NURSE Well, sir, my mistress is the sweetest lady. Lord,
> Lord! when 'twas a little prating thing – O, there is a
190 nobleman in town, one Paris, that would fain lay knife
191 aboard; but she, good soul, had as lieve see a toad, a
> very toad, as see him. I anger her sometimes, and tell her
> that Paris is the properer man; but I'll warrant you,
194 when I say so, she looks as pale as any clout in the versal
> world. Doth not rosemary and Romeo begin both with a
> letter?

ROMEO Ay, nurse; what of that? Both with an R.

197 NURSE Ah, mocker! that's the dog's name. R is for the -
> No; I know it begins with some other letter; and she
199 hath the prettiest sententious of it, of you and rosemary,
> that it would do you good to hear it.

ROMEO Commend me to thy lady.

NURSE Ay, a thousand times. *[Exit Romeo.]* Peter!

PETER Anon.

204 NURSE [Peter, take my fan, and go] before, and apace.
> *Exit [after Peter].*

*

II, v   *Enter Juliet.*

JULIET
> The clock struck nine when I did send the nurse;
> In half an hour she promised to return.
> Perchance she cannot meet him. That's not so.

190–91 *lay knife aboard* i.e. partake of this dish   191 *lieve* willingly   194 *clout* cloth; *versal* universal   197 *dog's name* (R was called 'the dog's letter,' since the sound 'r-r-r-r' supposedly resembles a dog's growl. The Nurse thinks it an ugly sound.)   199 *sententious* sentences   204 *Peter . . . go* (from Q1)
II, v The Capulet orchard

O, she is lame ! Love's heralds should be thoughts,
Which ten times faster glide than the sun's beams
Driving back shadows over low'ring hills.
Therefore do nimble-pinioned doves draw Love,   7
And therefore hath the wind-swift Cupid wings.
Now is the sun upon the highmost hill   9
Of this day's journey, and from nine till twelve
Is three long hours ; yet she is not come.
Had she affections and warm youthful blood,
She would be as swift in motion as a ball ;
My words would bandy her to my sweet love,   14
And his to me.
But old folks, many feign as they were dead –   16
Unwieldy, slow, heavy and pale as lead.
        Enter Nurse [and Peter].
O God, she comes ! O honey nurse, what news ?
Hast thou met with him ? Send thy man away.

NURSE
Peter, stay at the gate.   *[Exit Peter.]*

JULIET
Now, good sweet nurse – O Lord, why lookest thou sad ?
Though news be sad, yet tell them merrily ;
If good, thou shamest the music of sweet news
By playing it to me with so sour a face.

NURSE
I am aweary, give me leave awhile.   25
Fie, how my bones ache ! What a jaunce have I had !   26

JULIET
I would thou hadst my bones, and I thy news.
Nay, come, I pray thee speak. Good, good nurse, speak.

NURSE
Jesu, what haste ! Can you not stay awhile ?   29
Do you not see that I am out of breath ?

7 *nimble-pinioned* swift-winged; *doves* (Venus' birds, who draw her chariot)
9 *upon . . . hill* at the zenith   14 *bandy* speed, as in tennis   16 *old . . . dead*
many persons speak figuratively of old folks as being dead   25 *give me
leave* let me alone   26 *jaunce* j●lting   29 *stay* wait

JULIET
How art thou out of breath when thou hast breath
To say to me that thou art out of breath?
The excuse that thou dost make in this delay
Is longer than the tale thou dost excuse.
Is thy news good or bad? Answer to that.
36 Say either, and I'll stay the circumstance.
Let me be satisfied, is't good or bad?
38 NURSE Well, you have made a simple choice; you know
not how to choose a man. Romeo? No, not he. Though
his face be better than any man's, yet his leg excels all
men's; and for a hand and a foot, and a body, though
they be not to be talked on, yet they are past compare.
He is not the flower of courtesy, but, I'll warrant him, as
gentle as a lamb. Go thy ways, wench; serve God. What,
have you dined at home?

JULIET
No, no. But all this did I know before.
What says he of our marriage? What of that?

NURSE
Lord, how my head aches! What a head have I!
It beats as it would fall in twenty pieces.
50 My back a t' other side – ah, my back, my back!
51 Beshrew your heart for sending me about
To catch my death with jauncing up and down!

JULIET
I' faith, I am sorry that thou art not well.
Sweet, sweet, sweet nurse, tell me, what says my love?

NURSE Your love says, like an honest gentleman, and a
courteous, and a kind, and a handsome, and, I warrant,
a virtuous – Where is your mother?

JULIET
Where is my mother? Why, she is within.
Where should she be? How oddly thou repliest!

---

36 *stay the circumstance* wait for details 38 *simple* foolish 50 *a* on 51
Beshrew shame on

'Your love says, like an honest gentleman,
"Where is your mother?"'

NURSE   O God's Lady dear!
Are you so hot? Marry come up, I trow.   62
Is this the poultice for my aching bones?
Henceforward do your messages yourself.

JULIET
Here's such a coil! Come, what says Romeo?   65

NURSE
Have you got leave to go to shrift to-day?

JULIET
I have.

NURSE
Then hie you hence to Friar Laurence' cell;
There stays a husband to make you a wife.
Now comes the wanton blood up in your cheeks:
They'll be in scarlet straight at any news.   71
Hie you to church; I must another way,
To fetch a ladder, by the which your love
Must climb a bird's nest soon when it is dark.   74
I am the drudge, and toil in your delight;
But you shall bear the burden soon at night.
Go; I'll to dinner; hie you to the cell.

JULIET
Hie to high fortune! Honest nurse, farewell.   *Exeunt.*

*

Enter Friar [Laurence] and Romeo.   II, vi
FRIAR
So smile the heavens upon this holy act
That after-hours with sorrow chide us not!

62 *hot* angry; *Marry come up* by the Virgin Mary, take your come-uppance
(penalty); *trow* trust   65 *coil* fuss   71 *in scarlet* (Juliet blushes easily –
cf. II, ii, 86; III, ii, 14); *straight* straightway   74 *climb . . . nest* i.e. climb
to Juliet's room
II, vi Before Friar Laurence's cell

ROMEO

Amen, amen ! But come what sorrow can,
4   It cannot countervail the exchange of joy
That one short minute gives me in her sight.
Do thou but close our hands with holy words,
Then love-devouring death do what he dare –
It is enough I may but call her mine.

FRIAR

These violent delights have violent ends
And in their triumph die, like fire and powder,
Which, as they kiss, consume. The sweetest honey
12   Is loathsome in his own deliciousness
And in the taste confounds the appetite.
Therefore love moderately : long love doth so ;
15   Too swift arrives as tardy as too slow.

Enter Juliet.

Here comes the lady. O, so light a foot
17   Will ne'er wear out the everlasting flint.
18   A lover may bestride the gossamer
That idles in the wanton summer air,
20   And yet not fall ; so light is vanity.

JULIET

21   Good even to my ghostly confessor.

FRIAR

Romeo shall thank thee, daughter, for us both.

JULIET

23   As much to him, else is his thanks too much.

ROMEO

Ah, Juliet, if the measure of thy joy
25   Be heaped like mine, and that thy skill be more
26   To blazon it, then sweeten with thy breath

---

4 *countervail* outweigh   12 *Is loathsome* i.e. if eaten to excess   15 *Too . . .
slow* (proverbial; cf. II, iii, 94)   17 *wear . . . flint* (suggested by the proverb
'In time small water drops will wear away the stone')   18 *gossamer* spider's
web   20 *vanity* transitory earthly love (cf. Ecclesiastes ix, 9)   21 *ghostly*
spiritual   23 *As much* the same greeting   25 *that* if; *thy . . . more* you sing
better than I   26 *blazon* set forth

This neighbor air, and let rich music's tongue
Unfold the imagined happiness that both
Receive in either by this dear encounter.

JULIET

Conceit, more rich in matter than in words, 30
Brags of his substance, not of ornament.
They are but beggars that can count their worth;
But my true love is grown to such excess 33
I cannot sum up sum of half my wealth.

FRIAR

Come, come with me, and we will make short work;
For, by your leaves, you shall not stay alone
Till Holy Church incorporate two in one.   *[Exeunt.]*

*

Enter Mercutio, Benvolio, and Men. III, i

BENVOLIO

I pray thee, good Mercutio, let's retire.
The day is hot, the Capulets abroad,
And, if we meet, we shall not 'scape a brawl,
For now, these hot days, is the mad blood stirring.

MERCUTIO Thou art like one of these fellows that, when
he enters the confines of a tavern, claps me his sword
upon the table and says 'God send me no need of thee!'
and by the operation of the second cup draws him on 8
the drawer, when indeed there is no need.

BENVOLIO Am I like such a fellow?

MERCUTIO Come, come, thou art as hot a Jack in thy
mood as any in Italy; and as soon moved to be moody, 12
and as soon moody to be moved.

30–31 *Conceit . . . ornament* my understanding is fixed upon the reality of
my great love, not upon a vocal expression of it   33 *love . . . excess* (cf. II, ii,
135 and n.)
III, i A public place in Verona   8–9 *by the operation . . . drawer* after drinking
only two cups of wine, draws his sword against the waiter   12 *moody*
angry

BENVOLIO And what to?

MERCUTIO Nay, an there were two such, we should have
none shortly, for one would kill the other. Thou! why,
thou wilt quarrel with a man that hath a hair more or a
hair less in his beard than thou hast. Thou wilt quarrel
with a man for cracking nuts, having no other reason
but because thou hast hazel eyes. What eye but such an
21   eye would spy out such a quarrel? Thy head is as full of
quarrels as an egg is full of meat; and yet thy head hath
been beaten as addle as an egg for quarrelling. Thou
hast quarrelled with a man for coughing in the street,
because he hath wakened thy dog that hath lain asleep in
the sun. Didst thou not fall out with a tailor for wearing
27   his new doublet before Easter? with another for tying
28   his new shoes with old riband? And yet thou wilt tutor
me from quarrelling!

BENVOLIO An I were so apt to quarrel as thou art, any
31   man should buy the fee simple of my life for an hour and
a quarter.

33 MERCUTIO The fee simple? O simple!
          Enter Tybalt and others.

BENVOLIO By my head, here come the Capulets.

MERCUTIO By my heel, I care not.

TYBALT
    Follow me close, for I will speak to them.
37   Gentlemen, good-den. A word with one of you.

MERCUTIO
    And but one word with one of us?
    Couple it with something; make it a word and a blow.

TYBALT You shall find me apt enough to that, sir, an you
    will give me occasion.

MERCUTIO Could you not take some occasion without
    giving?

---

21 *spy out* see occasion for   27 *doublet* jacket   28 *riband* ribbon   31 *fee
simple* permanent lease   31–32 *hour and a quarter* probable duration of the
lease, i.e. of my life   33 *O simple* O stupid; **s.d.** (Q2 includes the name
'Petruchio')   37 *good-den* good afternoon

TYBALT Mercutio, thou consortest with Romeo.

MERCUTIO Consort? What, dost thou make us minstrels? 45
An thou make minstrels of us, look to hear nothing but
discords. Here's my fiddlestick; here's that shall make 47
you dance. Zounds, consort! 48

BENVOLIO
We talk here in the public haunt of men.
Either withdraw unto some private place,
Or reason coldly of your grievances,
Or else depart. Here all eyes gaze on us.

MERCUTIO
Men's eyes were made to look, and let them gaze.
I will not budge for no man's pleasure, I
Enter Romeo.

TYBALT
Well, peace be with you, sir. Here comes my man.

MERCUTIO
But I'll be hanged, sir, if he wear your livery. 56
Marry, go before to field, he'll be your follower! 57
Your worship in that sense may call him man.

TYBALT
Romeo, the love I bear thee can afford
No better term than this : thou art a villain.

ROMEO
Tybalt, the reason that I have to love thee
Doth much excuse the appertaining rage 62
To such a greeting. Villain am I none.
Therefore farewell. I see thou knowest me not

TYBALT
Boy, this shall not excuse the injuries
That thou hast done me ; therefore turn and draw.

---

45 *Consort* (1) associate with, (2) accompany in vocal or instrumental music;
minstrels (a more disreputable title than 'musicians'; cf. IV, v, 111–12)
47 *fiddlestick* i.e. rapier   **48** *Zounds* by God's wounds   **56** *livery* servant's
uniform (*my man* could mean 'my manservant')   **57** *field* duelling ground
62 *appertaining rage* suitably angry reaction

ROMEO
    I do protest I never injured thee,
68 But love thee better than thou canst devise
    Till thou shalt know the reason of my love;
70 And so, good Capulet, which name I tender
    As dearly as mine own, be satisfied.
MERCUTIO
    O calm, dishonorable, vile submission!
73 Alla stoccata carries it away.
        [Draws.]
    Tybalt, you ratcatcher, will you walk?
TYBALT
    What wouldst thou have with me?
MERCUTIO Good King of Cats, nothing but one of your
77 nine lives. That I mean to make bold withal, and, as you
78 shall use me hereafter, dry-beat the rest of the eight. Will
79 you pluck your sword out of his pilcher by the ears?
    Make haste, lest mine be about your ears ere it be out.
TYBALT I am for you.
        [Draws.]
ROMEO
    Gentle Mercutio, put thy rapier up.
83 MERCUTIO Come, sir, your passado!
        [They fight.]
ROMEO
    Draw, Benvolio; beat down their weapons.
    Gentlemen, for shame! forbear this outrage!
    Tybalt, Mercutio, the Prince expressly hath
    Forbid this bandying in Verona streets.
88 Hold, Tybalt! Good Mercutio!
        [Tybalt under Romeo's arm thrusts Mercutio in,
                    and flies with his Followers.]

68 *devise* understand   70 *tender* value   73 *Alla stoccata* 'at the thrust'; i.e.
Tybalt; *carries it away* triumphs, gets away with it   77 *nine lives* (proverbial: a cat has nine lives)   78 *dry-beat* thrash   79 *pilcher* scabbard   83
passado lunge   88 s.d. (from Q1; Q2 reads 'Away Tybalt.')

MERCUTIO   I am hurt.

    A plague a both your houses! I am sped.   89

    Is he gone and hath nothing?

BENVOLIO   What, art thou hurt?

MERCUTIO

    Ay, ay, a scratch, a scratch. Marry, 'tis enough.

    Where is my page? Go, villain, fetch a surgeon.

                            [Exit Page.]

ROMEO

    Courage, man. The hurt cannot be much.

MERCUTIO No, 'tis not so deep as a well, nor so wide as a

    church door; but 'tis enough, 'twill serve. Ask for me

    to-morrow, and you shall find me a grave man. I am 96

    peppered, I warrant, for this world. A plague a both

    your houses! Zounds, a dog, a rat, a mouse, a cat, to

    scratch a man to death! a braggart, a rogue, a villain,

    that fights by the book of arithmetic! Why the devil 100

    came you between us? I was hurt under your arm.

ROMEO

    I thought all for the best.

MERCUTIO

    Help me into some house, Benvolio,

    Or I shall faint. A plague a both your houses!

    They have made worms' meat of me. I have it,   105

    And soundly too. Your houses!

                 Exit [supported by Benvolio].

ROMEO

    This gentleman, the Prince's near ally,

    My very friend, hath got this mortal hurt   108

    In my behalf – my reputation stained

    With Tybalt's slander – Tybalt, that an hour

    Hath been my cousin. O sweet Juliet,

    Thy beauty hath made me effeminate

    And in my temper soft'ned valor's steel!

---

89 *a* on; *sped* mortally wounded   **96** *grave* (1) serious, (2) inhabiting a grave   **100** *by . . . arithmetic* by timing his strokes (cf. II, iv, 21)   **105** *worms' meat* i.e. a corpse; *I have it* I am wounded   **108** *very* true

Enter Benvolio.

BENVOLIO

O Romeo, Romeo, brave Mercutio is dead!

115   That gallant spirit hath aspired the clouds,

Which too untimely here did scorn the earth.

ROMEO

117   This day's black fate on moe days doth depend;

This but begins the woe others must end.

[Enter Tybalt.]

BENVOLIO

Here comes the furious Tybalt back again.

ROMEO

Alive in triumph, and Mercutio slain?

121   Away to heaven respective lenity,

122   And fire-eyed fury be my conduct now!

Now, Tybalt, take the 'villain' back again

That late thou gavest me; for Mercutio's soul

Is but a little way above our neads,

Staying for thine to keep him company.

Either thou or I, or both, must go with him.

TYBALT

Thou, wretched boy, that didst consort him here,

Shalt with him hence.

ROMEO   This shall determine that.

They fight. Tybalt falls.

BENVOLIO

Romeo, away, be gone!

The citizens are up, and Tybalt slain.

Stand not amazed. The Prince will doom thee death

If thou art taken. Hence, be gone, away!

ROMEO

134   O, I am fortune's fool!

BENVOLIO   Why dost thou stay? *Exit Romeo.*

---

115 *aspired* climbed toward   **117** *moe* more; *depend* hang down over (cf. I, iv, 107 and note)   **121** *respective lenity* reasoned gentleness (personified as an angel)   **122** *fire-eyed fury* (fury personified); *conduct* guide   **134** *fool* dupe, victim

Enter Citizens.

CITIZEN
Which way ran he that killed Mercutio?
Tybalt, that murderer, which way ran he?

BENVOLIO
There lies that Tybalt.

CITIZEN   Up, sir, go with me.
I charge thee in the Prince's name obey.
    Enter Prince [attended], old Montague, Capulet,
    their Wives, and all.

PRINCE
Where are the vile beginners of this fray?

BENVOLIO
O noble Prince, I can discover all   140
The unlucky manage of this fatal brawl.   141
There lies the man, slain by young Romeo,
That slew thy kinsman, brave Mercutio.

CAPULET'S WIFE
Tybalt, my cousin! O my brother's child!
O Prince! O husband! O, the blood is spilled
Of my dear kinsman! Prince, as thou art true,
For blood of ours shed blood of Montague.
O cousin, cousin!

PRINCE
Benvolio, who began this bloody fray?

BENVOLIO
Tybalt, here slain, whom Romeo's hand did slay.
Romeo, that spoke him fair, bid him bethink
How nice the quarrel was, and urged withal   152
Your high displeasure. All this – utterèd
With gentle breath, calm look, knees humbly bowed –
Could not take truce with the unruly spleen   155
Of Tybalt deaf to peace, but that he tilts
With piercing steel at bold Mercutio's breast;
Who, all as hot, turns deadly point to point,

140 *discover* reveal   141 *manage* course   152 *nice* trivial   155 *spleen* temper

And, with a martial scorn, with one hand beats
Cold death aside and with the other sends
It back to Tybalt, whose dexterity
Retorts it. Romeo, he cries aloud,
'Hold, friends! friends, part!' and swifter than his
   tongue,
His agile arm beats down their fatal points,
And 'twixt them rushes; underneath whose arm
166 An envious thrust from Tybalt hit the life
Of stout Mercutio, and then Tybalt fled;
But by and by comes back to Romeo,
169 Who had but newly entertained revenge,
And to't they go like lightning; for, ere I
Could draw to part them, was stout Tybalt slain;
And, as he fell, did Romeo turn and fly.
This is the truth, or let Benvolio die.

CAPULET'S WIFE
He is a kinsman to the Montague;
Affection makes him false, he speaks not true.
Some twenty of them fought in this black strife,
And all those twenty could but kill one life.
I beg for justice, which thou, Prince, must give.
Romeo slew Tybalt; Romeo must not live.

PRINCE
Romeo slew him; he slew Mercutio.
Who now the price of his dear blood doth owe?

MONTAGUE
Not Romeo, Prince; he was Mercutio's friend;
His fault concludes but what the law should end,
The life of Tybalt.

PRINCE   And for that offense
Immediately we do exile him hence.
I have an interest in your hate's proceeding,
My blood for your rude brawls doth lie a-bleeding;
188 But I'll amerce you with so strong a fine

166 *envious* malicious   169 *entertained* harbored thoughts of   188 *amerce* penalize

That you shall all repent the loss of mine.
I will be deaf to pleading and excuses;
Nor tears nor prayers shall purchase out abuses.
Therefore use none. Let Romeo hence in haste,
Else, when he is found, that hour is his last.
Bear hence this body, and attend our will.   194
Mercy but murders, pardoning those that kill.

Exit [with others].

*

Enter Juliet alone.   III, ii

JULIET

Gallop apace, you fiery-footed steeds,   1
Towards Phoebus' lodging! Such a wagoner   2
As Phaeton would whip you to the west   3
And bring in cloudy night immediately.
Spread thy close curtain, love-performing night,
That runaways' eyes may wink, and Romeo   6
Leap to these arms untalked of and unseen.
Lovers can see to do their amorous rites
By their own beauties; or, if love be blind,   9
It best agrees with night. Come, civil night,
Thou sober-suited matron, all in black,
And learn me how to lose a winning match,
Played for a pair of stainless maidenhoods.
Hood my unmanned blood, bating in my cheeks,   14
With thy black mantle till strange love grow bold,   15
Think true love acted simple modesty.   16
Come, night; come, Romeo; come, thou day in night;
For thou wilt lie upon the wings of night
Whiter than new snow upon a raven's back.
Come, gentle night; come, loving, black-browed night;

194 *attend our will* come to be judged
III, ii Capulet's house   1 *steeds* horses drawing the chariot of the sun
2 *Phoebus* the sun-god; *lodging* (below the western horizon)   3 *Phaeton*
Phoebus' son, with whom the horses of the sun ran away   6 *runaways' eyes*
eyes of the sun's horses (?); *wink* close   9 *love* Cupid   14 *Hood* cover with
a hood (falconry); *unmanned* untamed; *bating* fluttering   15 *strange* un-
familiar   16 *true love acted* the act of true love

Give me my Romeo; and, when he shall die,
Take him and cut him out in little stars,
And he will make the face of heaven so fine
That all the world will be in love with night
And pay no worship to the garish sun.
O, I have bought the mansion of a love,
But not possessed it; and though I am sold,
Not yet enjoyed. So tedious is this day
As is the night before some festival
30 To an impatient child that hath new robes
And may not wear them. O, here comes my nurse,
          Enter Nurse, with cords.
And she brings news; and every tongue that speaks
But Romeo's name speaks heavenly eloquence.
Now, nurse, what news? What hast thou there, the cords
That Romeo bid thee fetch?

NURSE   Ay, ay, the cords.
          [Throws them down.]

JULIET
Ay me! what news? Why dost thou wring thy hands?

NURSE
37 Ah, weraday! he's dead, he's dead, he's dead!
We are undone, lady, we are undone!
Alack the day! he's gone, he's killed, he's dead!

JULIET
40 Can heaven be so envious?

NURSE   Romeo can,
Though heaven cannot. O Romeo, Romeo!
Who ever would have thought it? Romeo!

JULIET
What devil art thou that dost torment me thus?
This torture should be roared in dismal hell.
45 Hath Romeo slain himself? Say thou but 'I,'
And that bare vowel 'I' shall poison more

---

37 *weraday* welladay, alas   40 *heaven . . . envious* (cf. III, v, 211)   45-50
I (with the alternate meaning 'ay')

Than the death-darting eye of cockatrice. 47
I am not I, if there be such an 'I'
Or those eyes' shot that makes the answer 'I.' 49
If he be slain, say 'I'; or if not, 'no.'
Brief sounds determine of my weal or woe.

NURSE

I saw the wound, I saw it with mine eyes,
(God save the mark!) here on his manly breast. 53
A piteous corse, a bloody piteous corse;
Pale, pale as ashes, all bedaubed in blood,
All in gore-blood. I swounded at the sight. 56

JULIET

O, break, my heart! poor bankrout, break at once! 57
To prison, eyes; ne'er look on liberty!
Vile earth, to earth resign; end motion here, 59
And thou and Romeo press one heavy bier!

NURSE-

O Tybalt, Tybalt, the best friend I had!
O courteous Tybalt! honest gentleman!
That ever I should live to see thee dead!

JULIET

What storm is this that blows so contrary?
Is Romeo slaught'red, and is Tybalt dead?
My dearest cousin, and my dearer lord?
Then, dreadful trumpet, sound the general doom! 67
For who is living, if those two are gone?

NURSE

Tybalt is gone, and Romeo banishèd;
Romeo that killed him, he is banishèd.

JULIET

O God! Did Romeo's hand shed Tybalt's blood?

---

47 *cockatrice* basilisk (a fabulous serpent which killed with eye-glances) 49 *those eyes' shot* the Nurse's eye-glance, which may inadvertently reveal her unspoken answer (see supplementary note on page 149) 53 *God . . . mark* God avert the evil omen 56 *gore-blood* clotted blood; *swounded* swooned 57 *bankrout* bankrupt 59 *Vile earth* i.e. my body; *resign* return 67 *trumpet* i.e. the 'last trumpet'; *general doom* Judgment Day

NURSE

72   It did, it did! alas the day, it did!

JULIET

73   O serpent heart, hid with a flow'ring face!
      Did ever dragon keep so fair a cave?

75   Beautiful tyrant! fiend angelical!

76   Dove-feathered raven! wolvish-ravening lamb!
      Despisèd substance of divinest show!
      Just opposite to what thou justly seem'st —
      A damnèd saint, an honorable villain!
      O nature, what hadst thou to do in hell

81   When thou didst bower the spirit of a fiend
      In mortal paradise of such sweet flesh?
      Was ever book containing such vile matter
      So fairly bound? O, that deceit should dwell
      In such a gorgeous palace!

NURSE   There's no trust,
      No faith, no honesty in men; all perjured,
      All forsworn, all naught, all dissemblers.

88   Ah, where's my man? Give me some aqua vitae.
      These griefs, these woes, these sorrows make me old.
      Shame come to Romeo!

JULIET   Blistered be thy tongue
      For such a wish! He was not born to shame.
      Upon his brow shame is ashamed to sit;
      For 'tis a throne where honor may be crowned
      Sole monarch of the universal earth.
      O, what a beast was I to chide at him!

NURSE

      Will you speak well of him that killed your cousin?

JULIET

      Shall I speak ill of him that is my husband?

72, 73 (in Q2 l. 72 is mistakenly assigned to Juliet, l. 73 to the Nurse)
73 *flow'ring face* (traditionally, the Serpent in Eden appeared to Eve with
the face of a young girl, wreathed in flowers)   **75** *fiend angelical* (cf. 2
Corinthians xi, 14)   **76** *wolvish-ravening lamb* (cf. Matthew vii, 15)
81–82 *spirit . . . paradise* i.e. the Serpent in Eden   **88** *aqua vitae* alcoholic
spirits

Ah, poor my lord, what tongue shall smooth thy name
When I, thy three-hours wife, have mangled it?
But wherefore, villain, didst thou kill my cousin?
That villain cousin would have killed my husband.
Back, foolish tears, back to your native spring!
Your tributary drops belong to woe,   103
Which you, mistaking, offer up to joy.
My husband lives, that Tybalt would have slain;
And Tybalt's dead, that would have slain my husband.
All this is comfort; wherefore weep I then?
Some word there was, worser than Tybalt's death,
That murd'red me. I would forget it fain;
But O, it presses to my memory
Like damnèd guilty deeds to sinners' minds!
'Tybalt is dead, and Romeo – banishèd.'
That 'banishèd,' that one word 'banishèd,'
Hath slain ten thousand Tybalts. Tybalt's death
Was woe enough, if it had ended there;
Or, if sour woe delights in fellowship
And needly will be ranked with other griefs,   117
Why followèd not, when she said 'Tybalt's dead,'
Thy father, or thy mother, nay, or both,
Which modern lamentation might have moved?   120
But with a rearward following Tybalt's death,   121
'Romeo is banishèd' – to speak that word
Is father, mother, Tybalt, Romeo, Juliet,
All slain, all dead. 'Romeo is banishèd' –
There is no end, no limit, measure, bound,
In that word's death; no words can that woe sound.
Where is my father and my mother, nurse?

NURSE
Weeping and wailing over Tybalt's corse.   128
Will you go to them? I will bring you thither.

JULIET
Wash they his wounds with tears? Mine shall be spent,

---

103 *tributary* tribute-paying   **117** *needly* necessarily   **120** *modern* ordinary, conventional   **121** *rearward* rearguard   **128** *corse* body

95

When theirs are dry, for Romeo's banishment.
Take up those cords. Poor ropes, you are beguiled,
Both you and I, for Romeo is exiled.
He made you for a highway to my bed;
But I, a maid, die maiden-widowèd.
Come, cords; come, nurse. I'll to my wedding bed;
And death, not Romeo, take my maidenhead!

NURSE

Hie to your chamber. I'll find Romeo
139   To comfort you. I wot well where he is.
Hark ye, your Romeo will be here at night.
I'll to him; he is hid at Laurence' cell.

JULIET

O, find him! give this ring to my true knight
And bid him come to take his last farewell.

                                        Exit [with Nurse].

                    *

III, iii   *Enter Friar [Laurence].*

FRIAR

1   Romeo, come forth; come forth, thou fearful man
2   Affliction is enamored of thy parts,
And thou art wedded to calamity.
            Enter Romeo.

ROMEO

Father, what news? What is the Prince's doom?
What sorrow craves acquaintance at my hand
That I yet know not?

FRIAR   Too familiar
Is my dear son with such sour company.
8   I bring thee tidings of the Prince's doom.

ROMEO

9   What less than doomsday is the Prince's doom?

---

139 *wot* know
III, iii Friar Laurence's cell   **s.d.** (separate entrances in Q1; Q2 reads 'Enter
Friar and Romeo.')   **1** *fearful* full of fear   **2** *parts* qualities   **8** *Prince's
doom* punishment decreed by the Prince   **9** *doomsday* i.e. death

RIAR
A gentler judgment vanished from his lips –   10
Not body's death, but body's banishment.

ROMEO
Ha, banishment? Be merciful, say 'death';
For exile hath more terror in his look,
Much more than death. Do not say 'banishment.'

FRIAR
Hence from Verona art thou banishèd.
Be patient, for the world is broad and wide.

ROMEO
There is no world without Verona walls,
But purgatory, torture, hell itself.
Hence banishèd is banished from the world,
And world's exile is death. Then 'banishèd'
Is death mistermed. Calling death 'banishèd,'
Thou cut'st my head off with a golden axe
And smilest upon the stroke that murders me.

FRIAR
O deadly sin! O rude unthankfulness!
Thy fault our law calls death; but the kind Prince,
Taking thy part, hath rushed aside the law,   26
And turned that black word 'death' to banishment.
This is dear mercy, and thou seest it not.

ROMEO
'Tis torture, and not mercy. Heaven is here,
Where Juliet lives; and every cat and dog
And little mouse, every unworthy thing,
Live here in heaven and may look on her;
But Romeo may not. More validity,   33
More honorable state, more courtship lives   34
In carrion flies than Romeo. They may seize
On the white wonder of dear Juliet's hand
And steal immortal blessing from her lips,
Who, even in pure and vestal modesty,   38

10 *vanished* disappeared into air   26 *rushed* pushed   33 *validity* value
34 *courtship* privilege of wooing   38 *vestal* virgin

39 Still blush, as thinking their own kisses sin ;
40 But Romeo may not, he is banishèd.
Flies may do this but I from this must fly ;
They are freemen, but I am banishèd.
And sayest thou yet that exile is not death ?
Hadst thou no poison mixed, no sharp-ground knife,
45 No sudden mean of death, though ne'er so mean,
But 'banishèd' to kill me – 'banishèd' ?
O friar, the damnèd use that word in hell :
Howling attends it ! How hast thou the heart,
Being a divine, a ghostly confessor,
A sin-absolver, and my friend professed,
To mangle me with that word 'banishèd' ?

FRIAR
52 Thou fond mad man, hear me a little speak.

ROMEO
O, thou wilt speak again of banishment.

FRIAR
I'll give thee armor to keep off that word ;
Adversity's sweet milk, philosophy,
To comfort thee, though thou art banishèd.

ROMEO
Yet 'banishèd' ? Hang up philosophy !
Unless philosophy can make a Juliet,
Displant a town, reverse a prince's doom,
It helps not, it prevails not. Talk no more.

FRIAR
O, then I see that madmen have no ears.

ROMEO
How should they, when that wise men have no eyes ?

FRIAR
63 Let me dispute with thee of thy estate.

39 *kisses* (when her lips touch each other) 40–42 (in Q2 these lines are preceded by 'This may flies do when I from this must fly' – evidently a cancelled line printed in error – and by l. 43, evidently misplaced) 45 *mean . . . mean* means . . . lowly 52 *fond* foolish 63 *dispute* reason; *estate* situation

ROMEO
  Thou canst not speak of that thou dost not feel.
  Wert thou as young as I, Juliet thy love,
  An hour but married, Tybalt murderèd,
  Doting like me, and like me banishèd,
  Then mightst thou speak, then mightst thou tear thy
      hair,
  And fall upon the ground, as I do now,
  Taking the measure of an unmade grave.   70
      Enter Nurse and knock.

FRIAR
  Arise; one knocks. Good Romeo, hide thyself.

ROMEO
  Not I; unless the breath of heartsick groans
  Mist-like infold me from the search of eyes.   73
      [Knock.]

FRIAR
  Hark, how they knock! Who's there? Romeo, arise;
  Thou wilt be taken. – Stay awhile! – Stand up;   75
      [Knock.]
  Run to my study. – By and by! – God's will,   76
  What simpleness is this. – I come, I come!   77
      Knock.
  Who knocks so hard? Whence come you? What's your
      will?
      Enter Nurse.

NURSE
  Let me come in, and you shall know my errand.
  I come from Lady Juliet.

FRIAR   Welcome then.

NURSE
  O holy friar, O, tell me, holy friar,
  Where is my lady's lord, where's Romeo?

70 *Taking the measure* providing the measurements; s.d. (so Q2, with another
entrance for Nurse at l. 78)   73 s.d. (Q2 reads 'They knock.')   75 s.d. (Q2
reads 'Slud knock.')   76 *By and by* in a moment   77 *simpleness* stupid
conduct

FRIAR
> There on the ground, with his own tears made drunk.

NURSE
> O, he is even in my mistress' case,
> Just in her case! O woeful sympathy!
> Piteous predicament! Even so lies she,
> Blubb'ring and weeping, weeping and blubb'ring.
> Stand up, stand up! Stand, an you be a man.
> For Juliet's sake, for her sake, rise and stand!
90 > Why should you fall into so deep an O?

ROMEO *[rises]* Nurse –

NURSE
> Ah sir! ah sir! Death's the end of all.

ROMEO
> Spakest thou of Juliet? How is it with her?
94 > Doth not she think me an old murderer,
> Now I have stained the childhood of our joy
> With blood removed but little from her own?
> Where is she? and how doth she! and what says
98 > My concealed lady to our cancelled love?

NURSE
> O, she says nothing, sir, but weeps and weeps;
> And now falls on her bed, and then starts up,
> And Tybalt calls; and then on Romeo cries,
> And then down falls again.

ROMEO   As if that name,
103 > Shot from the deadly level of a gun,
> Did murder her; as that name's cursèd hand
> Murdered her kinsman. O, tell me, friar, tell me,
106 > In what vile part of this anatomy
> Doth my name lodge? Tell me, that I may sack
108 > The hateful mansion.
> *[He offers to stab himself, and Nurse snatches the
> dagger away.]*

---

90 *an O* a fit of groaning   94 *old* hardened   98 *concealed ... cancelled* hidden
from me ... invalidated by my act (the two words were given almost the
same pronunciation)   103 *level* aim   106 *anatomy* body   108 s.d. (from Q1)

FRIAR   Hold thy desperate hand.
Art thou a man? Thy form cries out thou art;
Thy tears are womanish, thy wild acts denote
The unreasonable fury of a beast.   111
Unseemly woman in a seeming man!   112
And ill-beseeming beast in seeming both!   113
Thou hast amazed me. By my holy order,
I thought thy disposition better tempered.
Hast thou slain Tybalt? Wilt thou slay thyself?
And slay thy lady that in thy life lives,   117
By doing damnèd hate upon thyself?
Why railest thou on thy birth, the heaven, and earth?
Since birth and heaven and earth, all three do meet   120
In thee at once; which thou at once wouldst lose.
Fie, fie, thou shamest thy shape, thy love, thy wit,
Which, like a usurer, abound'st in all,   123
And usest none in that true use indeed   124
Which should bedeck thy shape, thy love, thy wit.
Thy noble shape is but a form of wax,   126
Digressing from the valor of a man;
Thy dear love sworn but hollow perjury,
Killing that love which thou hast vowed to cherish;   129
Thy wit, that ornament to shape and love,   130
Misshapen in the conduct of them both,   131
Like powder in a skilless soldier's flask,   132
Is set afire by thine own ignorance,
And thou dismemb'red with thine own defense   134
What, rouse thee, man! Thy Juliet is alive,
For whose dear sake thou wast but lately dead.   136
There art thou happy. Tybalt would kill thee,   137

---

111 *unreasonable* irrational   112 *Unseemly . . . seeming* disorderly . . . apparent   113 *ill-beseeming . . . both* inappropriate . . . man and woman   117 *in . . . lives* (cf. II, i, 1 and n.)   120 *all . . . meet* the soul comes from heaven, the body from earth; they unite in man at his birth   123 *Which* (you) who; *all* all capabilities   124 *true use* proper handling of wealth   126 *form of wax* waxwork, outward appearance   129 *Killing that love* (cf. l. 117)   130 *wit* intellect   131 *Misshapen* distorted; *conduct* guidance   132 *flask* powder horn   134 *defense* i.e. intellect   136 *dead* as one dead   137 *happy* fortunate

But thou slewest Tybalt. There art thou happy too.
The law, that threat'ned death, becomes thy friend
And turns it to exile. There art thou happy.
A pack of blessings light upon thy back;
Happiness courts thee in her best array;
But, like a misbehaved and sullen wench,
Thou pout'st upon thy fortune and thy love.
Take heed, take heed, for such die miserable.
Go get thee to thy love, as was decreed,
Ascend her chamber, hence and comfort her.
But look thou stay not till the watch be set,
For then thou canst not pass to Mantua,
Where thou shalt live till we can find a time
151   To blaze your marriage, reconcile your friends,
Beg pardon of the Prince, and call thee back
With twenty hundred thousand times more joy
Than thou went'st forth in lamentation.
Go before, nurse. Commend me to thy lady,
And bid her hasten all the house to bed,
Which heavy sorrow makes them apt unto.
Romeo is coming.

NURSE

O Lord, I could have stayed here all the night
To hear good counsel. O, what learning is!
My lord, I'll tell my lady you will come.

ROMEO

Do so, and biα my sweet prepare to chide.

NURSE

Here is a ring she bid me give you, sir.
Hie you, make haste, for it grows very late.   *[Exit.]*

ROMEO

How well my comfort is revived by this!

FRIAR

166   Go hence; good night; and here stands all your state:
Either be gone before the watch be set,

151 *blaze* publish   166 *here . . . state* here is your situation

Or by the break of day disguised from hence.
Sojourn in Mantua. I'll find out your man,
And he shall signify from time to time
Every good hap to you that chances here.
Give me thy hand. 'Tis late. Farewell; good night.

ROMEO

But that a joy past joy calls out on me,
It were a grief so brief to part with thee.
Farewell.   *Exeunt.*

*

Enter old Capulet, his Wife, and Paris.   III, iv

CAPULET

Things have fall'n out, sir, so unluckily
That we have had no time to move our daughter.   2
Look you, she loved her kinsman Tybalt dearly,
And so did I. Well, we were born to die.
'Tis very late; she'll not come down to-night.
I promise you, but for your company,
I would have been abed an hour ago.

PARIS

These times of woe afford no times to woo.
Madam, good night. Commend me to your daughter.

LADY

I will, and know her mind early to-morrow;
To-night she's mewed up to her heaviness.   11

CAPULET

Sir Paris, I will make a desperate tender   12
Of my child's love. I think she will be ruled
In all respects by me; nay more, I doubt it not.
Wife, go you to her ere you go to bed;
Acquaint her here of my son Paris' love
And bid her (mark you me?) on Wednesday next –
But soft! what day is this?

PARIS   Monday, my lord.

III, iv Capulet's house   2 *move* talk with   11 *mewed up* shut up (falconry);
heaviness grief   12 *desperate tender* risk-taking offer

CAPULET
> Monday ! ha, ha ! Well, Wednesday is too soon.
20   A Thursday let it be – a Thursday, tell her,
> She shall be married to this noble earl.
> Will you be ready ? Do you like this haste ?
> We'll keep no great ado – a friend or two ;
> For hark you, Tybalt being slain so late,
> It may be thought we held him carelessly,
> Being our kinsman, if we revel much.
> Therefore we'll have some half a dozen friends,
> And there an end. But what say you to Thursday ?

PARIS
> My lord, I would that Thursday were to-morrow.

CAPULET
> Well, get you gone. A Thursday be it then.
> Go you to Juliet ere you go to bed ;
> Prepare her, wife, against this wedding day.
> Farewell, my lord. – Light to my chamber, ho !
34   Afore me, it is so very very late
35   That we may call it early by and by.
> Good night.   *Exeunt.*

*

III, v   *Enter Romeo and Juliet aloft [at the window].*

JULIET
> Wilt thou be gone ? It is not yet near day.
> It was the nightingale, and not the lark,
3   That pierced the fearful hollow of thine ear.
> Nightly she sings on yond pomegranate tree.
> Believe me, love, it was the nightingale.

ROMEO
> It was the lark, the herald of the morn ;
> No nightingale. Look, love, what envious streaks

20 *A* on   34 *Afore me* (a light oath)   35 *by and by* immediately
III, v The Capulet orchard   **s.d.** *at the window* (from Q1)   3 *fearful* apprehensive

Do lace the severing clouds in yonder East.
Night's candles are burnt out, and jocund day 9
Stands tiptoe on the misty mountain tops.
I must be gone and live, or stay and die.

JULIET
Yond light is not daylight; I know it, I.
It is some meteor that the sun exhales 13
To be to thee this night a torchbearer
And light thee on thy way to Mantua.
Therefore stay yet; thou need'st not to be gone.

ROMEO
Let me be ta'en, let me be put to death.
I am content, so thou wilt have it so.
I'll say yon grey is not the morning's eye,
'Tis but the pale reflex of Cynthia's brow; 20
Nor that is not the lark whose notes do beat
The vaulty heaven so high above our heads.
I have more care to stay than will to go.
Come, death, and welcome! Juliet wills it so.
How is't, my soul? Let's talk; it is not day. 25

JULIET
It is, it is! Hie hence, be gone, away!
It is the lark that sings so out of tune,
Straining harsh discords and unpleasing sharps.
Some say the lark makes sweet division; 29
This doth not so, for she divideth us.
Some say the lark and loathèd toad change eyes; 31
O, now I would they had changed voices too,
Since arm from arm that voice doth us affray, 33
Hunting thee hence with hunt's-up to the day. 34
O, now be gone! More light and light it grows.

9 *Night's candles* the stars 13 *meteor* nocturnal light, such as the will-o'-the-wisp, supposedly of luminous gas given off by the sun or drawn by his power (*exhales*) out of marshy ground 20 *reflex . . . brow* reflection of the moon 25 *my soul* (cf. II, ii, 165) 29 *division* melody 31 *change* exchange (a folk belief) 33 *affray* frighten 34 *hunt's-up* morning song to awaken huntsmen

ROMEO

36   More light and light – more dark and dark our woes.
          Enter Nurse [hastily].

NURSE Madam!

JULIET Nurse?

NURSE

       Your lady mother is coming to your chamber.
       The day is broke; be wary, look about.   *[Exit.]*

JULIET

41   Then, window, let day in, and let life out.

ROMEO

42   Farewell, farewell! One kiss, and I'll descend.
          [He goeth down.]

JULIET

43   Art thou gone so, love-lord, ay husband-friend?
       I must hear from thee every day in the hour,
       For in a minute there are many days.

46   O, by this count I shall be much in years
       Ere I again behold my Romeo!

ROMEO

       Farewell!
       I will omit no opportunity
       That may convey my greetings, love, to thee.

JULIET

       O, think'st thou we shall ever meet again?

ROMEO

       I doubt it not; and all these woes shall serve
       For sweet discourses in our times to come.

JULIET

54   O God, I have an ill-divining soul!
       Methinks I see thee, now thou art so low,
       As one dead in the bottom of a tomb.
       Either my eyesight fails, or thou lookest pale.

---

36 s.d. *hastily* (from Q1; Q2 reads 'Enter Madam and Nurse.')   **41** *life* (cf. III, iii, 117)   **42 s.d.** (from Q1)   **43** *friend* clandestine lover   **46** *much* advanced   **54** *ill-divining* prophetic of evil

ROMEO
> And trust me, love, in my eye so do you.
> Dry sorrow drinks our blood. Adieu, adieu !   *Exit.* 59

JULIET
> O Fortune, Fortune ! all men call thee fickle.
> If thou art fickle, what dost thou with him
> That is renowned for faith ? Be fickle, Fortune,
> For then I hope thou wilt not keep him long
> But send him back.   64
> *[She goeth down from the window.]*
> *Enter Mother.*

LADY
> Ho, daughter ! are you up ?

JULIET
> Who is't that calls ? It is my lady mother.
> Is she not down so late, or up so early ?   67
> What unaccustomed cause procures her hither ?

LADY
> Why, how now, Juliet ?

JULIET   Madam, I am not well.

LADY
> Evermore weeping for your cousin's death ?
> What, wilt thou wash him from his grave with tears ?
> An if thou couldst, thou couldst not make him live.
> Therefore have done. Some grief shows much of love ;
> But much of grief shows still some want of wit.

JULIET
> Yet let me weep for such a feeling loss.   75

LADY
> So shall you feel the loss, but not the friend
> Which you weep for.

---

59 *Dry . . . blood* (the presumed effect of grief was to dry up the blood) **64**
s.d. (from Q1, and so placed that it might apply only to the Nurse; but since
the Q1 stage direction immediately following is 'Enter Juliet's Mother,
Nurse,' the indications are that the subsequent action takes place below,
where Juliet joins her mother; hence the orchard into which Romeo has de-
scended now becomes an interior) **67** *down* abed **75** *feeling* deeply felt

JULIET   Feeling so the loss,
I cannot choose but ever weep the friend.

LADY
Well, girl, thou weep'st not so much for his death
As that the villain lives which slaughtered him.

JULIET
What villain, madam ?

LADY   That same villain Romeo.

JULIET *[aside]*
Villain and he be many miles asunder. –
God pardon him ! I do, with all my heart ;

84 And yet no man like he doth grieve my heart.

LADY
That is because the traitor murderer lives.

JULIET
Ay, madam, from the reach of these my hands.
Would none but I might venge my cousin's death !

LADY
We will have vengeance for it, fear thou not.
Then weep no more. I'll send to one in Mantua,

90 Where that same banished runagate doth live,
Shall give him such an unaccustomed dram
That he shall soon keep Tybalt company ;
And then I hope thou wilt be satisfied.

JULIET
Indeed I never shall be satisfied
With Romeo till I behold him – dead –
Is my poor heart so for a kinsman vexed.
Madam, if you could find out but a man

98 To bear a poison, I would temper it ;
That Romeo should, upon receipt thereof,
Soon sleep in quiet. O, how my heart abhors
To hear him named and cannot come to him,
To wreak the love I bore my cousin
Upon his body that hath slaughtered him !

84 *like* so much as   **90** *runagate* renegade   **98** *temper* prepare or concoct
(with play on 'moderate')

LADY
> Find thou the means, and I'll find such a man.
> But now I'll tell thee joyful tidings, girl.

JULIET
> And joy comes well in such a needy time.
> What are they, beseech your ladyship?

LADY
> Well, well, thou hast a careful father, child;
> One who, to put thee from thy heaviness,
> Hath sorted out a sudden day of joy   110
> That thou expects not nor I looked not for.

JULIET
> Madam, in happy time! What day is that?   112

LADY
> Marry, my child, early next Thursday morn
> The gallant, young, and noble gentleman,
> The County Paris, at Saint Peter's Church,
> Shall happily make thee there a joyful bride.

JULIET
> Now by Saint Peter's Church, and Peter too,
> He shall not make me there a joyful bride!
> I wonder at this haste, that I must wed
> Ere he that should be husband comes to woo.
> I pray you tell my lord and father, madam,
> I will not marry yet; and when I do, I swear
> It shall be Romeo, whom you know I hate,
> Rather than Paris. These are news indeed!

LADY
> Here comes your father. Tell him so yourself,
> And see how he will take it at your hands.
> *Enter Capulet and Nurse.*

CAPULET
> When the sun sets the earth doth drizzle dew,
> But for the sunset of my brother's son
> It rains downright.

110 *sorted* chosen   112 *in happy time* opportunely

130 How now? a conduit, girl? What, still in tears?
Evermore show'ring? In one little body
Thou counterfeit'st a bark, a sea, a wind:
For still thy eyes, which I may call the sea,
Do ebb and flow with tears; the bark thy body is,
Sailing in this salt flood; the winds, thy sighs,
Who, raging with thy tears and they with them,
137 Without a sudden calm will overset
Thy tempest-tossèd body. How now, wife?
Have you deliverèd to her our decree?

LADY

140 Ay, sir; but she will none, she gives you thanks.
141 I would the fool were married to her grave!

CAPULET

142 Soft! take me with you, take me with you, wife.
How? Will she none? Doth she not give us thanks?
Is she not proud? Doth she not count her blest,
145 Unworthy as she is, that we have wrought
146 So worthy a gentleman to be her bride?

JULIET

Not proud you have, but thankful that you have.
Proud can I never be of what I hate,
But thankful even for hate that is meant love.

CAPULET

150 How, how, how, how, chopped-logic? What is this?
'Proud'—and 'I thank you'—and 'I thank you not'—
And yet 'not proud'? Mistress minion you,
Thank me no thankings, nor proud me no prouds,
154 But fettle your fine joints 'gainst Thursday next
To go with Paris to Saint Peter's Church,
156 Or I will drag thee on a hurdle thither.

---

130 *conduit* water pipe   **137** *sudden* immediate   **140** *gives you thanks* says
'No, thank you'   **141** *married . . . grave* (a petulant but prophetic comment,
like l. 167 below)   **142** *take . . . you* let me understand you   **145** *wrought*
arranged for   **146** *bride* bridegroom   **150** *chopped-logic* hair-splitting   **154**
fettle prepare   **156** *hurdle* sledge on which criminals were carried to
execution

Out, you green-sickness carrion! out, you baggage!   157
You tallow-face!   158

LADY   Fie, fie! what, are you mad?

JULIET
Good father, I beseech you on my knees,
Hear me with patience but to speak a word.

CAPULET
Hang thee, young baggage! disobedient wretch!
I tell thee what – get thee to church a Thursday   162
Or never after look me in the face.
Speak not, reply not, do not answer me!
My fingers itch. Wife, we scarce thought us blest
That God had lent us but this only child;
But now I see this one is one too much,
And that we have a curse in having her.
Out on her, hilding!   169

NURSE   God in heaven bless her!
You are to blame, my lord, to rate her so.   170

CAPULET
And why, my Lady Wisdom? Hold your tongue,
Good Prudence. Smatter with your gossips, go!   172

NURSE
I speak no treason.

CAPULET   O, God-i-god-en!   173

NURSE
May not one speak?

CAPULET   Peace, you mumbling fool!
Utter your gravity o'er a gossip's bowl,
For here we need it not.

LADY   You are too hot.

CAPULET
God's bread! it makes me mad.   177

---

157 *green-sickness* anemic; *baggage* worthless woman **158** *tallow-face*
pale-face; *are you mad* (addressed to Capulet) **162** *a* on **169** *hilding*
worthless creature **170** *rate* scold **172** *Smatter . . . gossips* chatter with
your cronies **173** *God-i-god-en* for God's sake **177** *bread* bread of the
Sacrament

178　Day, night; hour, tide, time; work, play;
　　　Alone, in company; still my care hath been
　　　To have her matched; and having now provided
　　　A gentleman of noble parentage,
182　Of fair demesnes, youthful, and nobly trained,
　　　Stuffed, as they say, with honorable parts,
　　　Proportioned as one's thought would wish a man –
185　And then to have a wretched puling fool,
186　A whining mammet, in her fortune's tender,
　　　To answer 'I'll not wed, I cannot love;
　　　I am too young, I pray you pardon me'!
189　But, an you will not wed, I'll pardon you!
　　　Graze where you will, you shall not house with me.
191　Look to't, think on't; I do not use to jest.
192　Thursday is near; lay hand on heart, advise:
　　　An you be mine, I'll give you to my friend;
　　　An you be not, hang, beg, starve, die in the streets,
　　　For, by my soul, I'll ne'er acknowledge thee,
　　　Nor what is mine shall never do thee good.
　　　Trust to't. Bethink you. I'll not be forsworn.　　　*Exit.*

JULIET
　　　Is there no pity sitting in the clouds
　　　That sees into the bottom of my grief?
　　　O sweet my mother, cast me not away!
　　　Delay this marriage for a month, a week;
　　　Or if you do not, make the bridal bed
　　　In that dim monument where Tybalt lies.

LADY
　　　Talk not to me, for I'll not speak a word.
　　　Do as thou wilt, for I have done with thee.　　　*Exit.*

JULIET
　　　O God! – O nurse, how shall this be prevented?

178–79 *Day . . . company* (in Q1 the equivalent matter occupies two separate
lines: ' Day, night; early, late; at home, abroad: Alone, in company;
waking or sleeping;' – more logical, but irreconcilable with the Q2 passage
except by guesswork)　182 *demesnes* domains　185 *puling* whining　186
mammet doll; *tender* offer　189 *I'll pardon you* (ironic)　191 *do not use* am
not accustomed　192 *advise* consider

My husband is on earth, my faith in heaven.   207
How shall that faith return again to earth   208
Unless that husband send it me from heaven
By leaving earth? Comfort me, counsel me.
Alack, alack, that heaven should practise stratagems
Upon so soft a subject as myself!
What say'st thou? Hast thou not a word of joy?
Some comfort, nurse.

NURSE   Faith, here it is.
Romeo is banished; and all the world to nothing   215
That he dares ne'er come back to challenge you;   216
Or if he do, it needs must be by stealth.
Then, since the case so stands as now it doth,
I think it best you married with the County.
O, he's a lovely gentleman!
Romeo's a dishclout to him. An eagle, madam,   221
Hath not so green, so quick, so fair an eye
As Paris hath. Beshrew my very heart,
I think you are happy in this second match,
For it excels your first; or if it did not,
Your first is dead – or 'twere as good he were
As living here and you no use of him.

JULIET
Speak'st thou from thy heart?

NURSE
And from my soul too; else beshrew them both.   229

JULIET Amen!

NURSE What?

JULIET
Well, thou hast comforted me marvellous much.
Go in; and tell my lady I am gone,
Having displeased my father, to Laurence' cell,
To make confession and to be absolved.

---

207 *my faith in heaven* my marriage vow is recorded in heaven   **208–10** *How
... earth* how can I marry unless I am first widowed   **215** *all . . nothing* i.e.
it is a safe bet   **216** *challenge* demand possession of   **221** *dishclout* dishcloth
229 *beshrew* a curse on

NURSE
Marry, I will ; and this is wisely done.   *[Exit.]*
JULIET
237   Ancient damnation ! O most wicked fiend !
Is it more sin to wish me thus forsworn,
Or to dispraise my lord with that same tongue
Which she hath praised him with above compare
So many thousand times ? Go, counsellor !
242   Thou and my bosom henceforth shall be twain.
I'll to the friar to know his remedy.
If all else fail, myself have power to die.   *Exit.*

*

IV, i   *Enter Friar [Laurence] and County Paris.*

FRIAR
On Thursday, sir ? The time is very short.
PARIS
My father Capulet will have it so,
And I am nothing slow to slack his haste.
FRIAR
You say you do not know the lady's mind.
5   Uneven is the course ; I like it not.
PARIS
Immoderately she weeps for Tybalt's death,
And therefore have I little talked of love ;
8   For Venus smiles not in a house of tears.
Now, sir, her father counts it dangerous
That she do give her sorrow so much sway,
And in his wisdom hastes our marriage
To stop the inundation of her tears,
13   Which, too much minded by herself alone,

237 *Ancient damnation* damnable old woman   242 *bosom* confidence; *twain*
separated
IV, i Friar Laurence's cell   5 *course* i.e. racecourse   8 *Venus . . . tears* the
influence of the planet Venus is unfavorable when she appears in the 'house'
of a 'moist' constellation, such as Pisces or Aquarius; i.e. one cannot talk of
love amidst grief   13 *minded* thought about

May be put from her by society.
Now do you know the reason of this haste.

FRIAR [aside]
I would I knew not why it should be slowed. –
Look, sir, here comes the lady toward my cell.
        Enter Juliet.

PARIS
Happily met, my lady and my wife!

JULIET
That may be, sir, when I may be a wife.

PARIS
That 'may be' must be, love, on Thursday next.   20

JULIET
What must be shall be.

FRIAR   That's a certain text.

PARIS
Come you to make confession to this father?

JULIET
To answer that, I should confess to you.

PARIS
Do not deny to him that you love me.

JULIET
I will confess to you that I love him.

PARIS
So will ye, I am sure, that you love me.

JULIET
If I do so, it will be of more price,
Being spoke behind your back, than to your face.

PARIS
Poor soul, thy face is much abused with tears.

JULIET
The tears have got small victory by that,   30
For it was bad enough before their spite.

PARIS
Thou wrong'st it more than tears with that report.

JULIET
That is no slander, sir, which is a truth;

And what I spake, I spake it to my face.

PARIS

Thy face is mine, and thou hast sland'red it.

JULIET

It may be so, for it is not mine own.
Are you at leisure, holy father, now,
Or shall I come to you at evening mass?

FRIAR

My leisure serves me, pensive daughter, now.
My lord, we must entreat the time alone.

PARIS

41   God shield I should disturb devotion!
Juliet, on Thursday early will I rouse ye.
Till then, adieu, and keep this holy kiss.   *Exit*.

JULIET

O, shut the door! and when thou hast done so,
Come weep with me – past hope, past cure, past help!

FRIAR

Ah, Juliet, I already know thy grief;
47   It strains me past the compass of my wits.
48   I hear thou must, and nothing may prorogue it,
On Thursday next be married to this County.

JULIET

Tell me not, friar, that thou hearest of this,
Unless thou tell me how I may prevent it.
If in thy wisdom thou canst give no help,
Do thou but call my resolution wise
And with this knife I'll help it presently.
God joined my heart and Romeo's, thou our hands;
And ere this hand, by thee to Romeo's sealed,
57   Shall be the label to another deed,
Or my true heart with treacherous revolt
Turn to another, this shall slay them both.
60   Therefore, out of thy long-experienced time,

---

41 *shield* forbid   47 *the compass . . . wits* my wit's end   48 *prorogue* postpone
57 *label* i.e. strip of parchment bearing the seal, attached to a deed   60 *time*
age

Give me some present counsel; or, behold,
'Twixt my extremes and me this bloody knife   62
Shall play the umpire, arbitrating that
Which the commission of thy years and art   64
Could to no issue of true honor bring.
Be not so long to speak. I long to die
If what thou speak'st speak not of remedy.

FRIAR

Hold, daughter. I do spy a kind of hope,
Which craves as desperate an execution
As that is desperate which we would prevent.
If, rather than to marry County Paris,
Thou hast the strength of will to slay thyself,
Then it is likely thou wilt undertake
A thing like death to chide away this shame,
That cop'st with death himself to scape from it;   75
And, if thou darest, I'll give thee remedy.

JULIET

O, bid me leap, rather than marry Paris,
From off the battlements of any tower,
Or walk in thievish ways, or bid me lurk   79
Where serpents are; chain me with roaring bears,
Or hide me nightly in a charnel house,   81
O'ercovered quite with dead men's rattling bones,
With reeky shanks and yellow chapless skulls;   83
Or bid me go into a new-made grave
And hide me with a dead man in his shroud –
Things that, to hear them told, have made me tremble –
And I will do it without fear or doubt,
To live an unstained wife to my sweet love.

FRIAR

Hold, then. Go home, be merry, give consent
To marry Paris. Wednesday is to-morrow.

---

62 *extremes* difficulties   **64** *commission . . . art* authority of your age and skill
75 *cop'st* encounterest   **79** *thievish ways* roads frequented by robbers   **81**
charnel house depository of human bones   **83** *reeky* smelly; *chapless* jawless

To-morrow night look that thou lie alone;
Let not the nurse lie with thee in thy chamber.
Take thou this vial, being then in bed,
94 And this distilling liquor drink thou off;
When presently through all thy veins shall run
96 A cold and drowsy humor; for no pulse
97 Shall keep his native progress, but surcease;
No warmth, no breath, shall testify thou livest;
The roses in thy lips and cheeks shall fade
100 To wanny ashes, thy eyes' windows fall
Like death when he shuts up the day of life;
102 Each part, deprived of supple government,
Shall, stiff and stark and cold, appear like death;
And in this borrowèd likeness of shrunk death
Thou shalt continue two-and-forty hours,
And then awake as from a pleasant sleep.
Now, when the bridegroom in the morning comes
To rouse thee from thy bed, there art thou dead.
Then, as the manner of our country is,
In thy best robes uncoverèd on the bier
111 Thou shalt be borne to that same ancient vault
Where all the kindred of the Capulets lie.
113 In the mean time, against thou shalt awake,
114 Shall Romeo by my letters know our drift;
And hither shall he come; and he and I
Will watch thy waking, and that very night
Shall Romeo bear thee hence to Mantua.
And this shall free thee from this present shame,
119 If no inconstant toy nor womanish fear
Abate thy valor in the acting it.

---

94 *distilling* infusing 96 *humor* moisture 97 *surcease* cease 100 *wanny* pale, shrunken; *windows* i.e. eyelids (the figure derives from the covering of shop-fronts at the close of the day) 102 *supple government* the life force that keeps the body supple 111 (in Q2 this line is preceded by 'Be borne to burial in thy kindred's grave,' evidently a cancelled version of the line, printed in error) 113 *against . . awake* in preparation for your awaking 114 *drift* intention 119 *toy* whim

JULIET
    Give me, give me! O, tell not me of fear!
FRIAR
    Hold! Get you gone, be strong and prosperous
    In this resolve. I'll send a friar with speed
    To Mantua, with my letters to thy lord.
JULIET
    Love give me strength! and strength shall help afford.
    Farewell, dear father.   *Exit [with Friar].*

                              *

    Enter Father Capulet, Mother, Nurse, and   IV, ii
    Servingmen, two or three.
CAPULET
    So many guests invite as here are writ.
                              [Exit a Servingman.]
    Sirrah, go hire me twenty cunning cooks.
SERVINGMAN   You shall have none ill, sir; for I'll try if
    they can lick their fingers.
CAPULET
    How canst thou try them so?   5
SERVINGMAN   Marry, sir, 'tis an ill cook that cannot lick 6
    his own fingers. Therefore he that cannot lick his fingers
    goes not with me.
CAPULET   Go, begone.   *[Exit Servingman.]*
    We shall be much unfurnished for this time.   10
    What, is my daughter gone to Friar Laurence?
NURSE   Ay, forsooth.
CAPULET
    Well, he may chance to do some good on her.
    A peevish self-willed harlotry it is.   14

IV, ii Capulet's house   5 *try* test   6–7 *'tis ... fingers* it's a poor cook who
doesn't like to taste the food which he prepares (proverbial)   10 *unfurnished*
unprovided   14 *harlotry* hussy

Enter Juliet.

NURSE
See where she comes from shrift with merry look.

CAPULET
How now, my headstrong? Where have you been gadding?

JULIET
Where I have learnt me to repent the sin
Of disobedient opposition
To you and your behests, and am enjoined
By holy Laurence to fall prostrate here
To beg your pardon. Pardon, I beseech you!
Henceforward I am ever ruled by you.

CAPULET
Send for the County. Go tell him of this.
24   I'll have this knot knit up to-morrow morning.

JULIET
I met the youthful lord at Laurence' cell
And gave him what becomèd love I might,
Not stepping o'er the bounds of modesty.

CAPULET
Why, I am glad on't. This is well. Stand up.
This is as't should be. Let me see the County.
Ay, marry, go, I say, and fetch him hither.
Now, afore God, this reverend holy friar,
32   All our whole city is much bound to him.

JULIET
Nurse, will you go with me into my closet
To help me sort such needful ornaments
As you think fit to furnish me to-morrow?

MOTHER
No, not till Thursday. There is time enough.

CAPULET
Go, nurse, go with her. We'll to church to-morrow.
                              Exeunt [Juliet and Nurse].

24 *to-morrow morning* (i.e. Wednesday, one day earlier than planned)   32
bound indebted

MOTHER
    We shall be short in our provision.
    'Tis now near night.
CAPULET   Tush, I will stir about,
    And all things shall be well, I warrant thee, wife.
    Go thou to Juliet, help to deck up her.
    I'll not to bed to-night; let me alone.
    I'll play the housewife for this once. What, ho!
    They are all forth; well, I will walk myself
    To County Paris, to prepare up him
    Against to-morrow. My heart is wondrous light,
    Since this same wayward girl is so reclaimed.
                             Exit [with Mother].

                   *

    Enter Juliet and Nurse.   IV, iii

JULIET
    Ay, those attires are best; but, gentle nurse,
    I pray thee leave me to myself to-night;
    For I have need of many orisons   3
    To move the heavens to smile upon my state,
    Which, well thou knowest, is cross and full of sin.   5
       Enter Mother.

MOTHER
    What, are you busy, ho? Need you my help?
JULIET
    No, madam; we have culled such necessaries   7
    As are behoveful for our state to-morrow.   8
    So please you, let me now be left alone,
    And let the nurse this night sit up with you;
    For I am sure you have your hands full all
    In this so sudden business.
MOTHER   Good night.
    Get thee to bed, and rest; for thou hast need.
                       Exeunt [Mother and Nurse].

IV, iii Juliet's chamber   3 *orisons* prayers   5 *cross* perverse   7 *culled*
picked out   8 *behoveful* fitting; *state* ceremony

JULIET

Farewell! God knows when we shall meet again.
15 I have a faint cold fear thrills through my veins
That almost freezes up the heat of life.
I'll call them back again to comfort me.
Nurse! – What should she do here?
My dismal scene I needs must act alone.
Come, vial.
What if this mixture do not work at all?
Shall I be married then to-morrow morning?
No, no! This shall forbid it. Lie thou there.
[Lays down a dagger.]
What if it be a poison which the friar
25 Subtly hath minist'red to have me dead,
Lest in this marriage he should be dishonored
Because he married me before to Romeo?
I fear it is; and yet methinks it should not,
29 For he hath still been tried a holy man.
How if, when I am laid into the tomb,
I wake before the time that Romeo
Come to redeem me? There's a fearful point!
Shall I not then be stifled in the vault,
To whose foul mouth no healthsome air breathes in,
And there die strangled ere my Romeo comes?
Or, if I live, is it not very like
37 The horrible conceit of death and night,
Together with the terror of the place –
As in a vault, an ancient receptacle
Where for this many hundred years the bones
Of all my buried ancestors are packed;
42 Where bloody Tybalt, yet but green in earth,
Lies fest'ring in his shroud; where, as they say,
At some hours in the night spirits resort –
45 Alack, alack, is it not like that I,

15 *faint* causing faintness   25 *minist'red* administered   29 *tried* proved
(after this line, Q1 inserts 'I will not entertain so bad a thought')   37 *conceit*
imagination   42 *green* new   45 *like* likely

So early waking – what with loathsome smells,
And shrieks like mandrakes torn out of the earth,   47
That living mortals, hearing them, run mad –
O, if I wake, shall I not be distraught,
Environèd with all these hideous fears,
And madly play with my forefathers' joints,
And pluck the mangled Tybalt from his shroud,
And, in this rage, with some great kinsman's bone
As with a club dash out my desp'rate brains ?
O, look ! methinks I see my cousin's ghost
Seeking out Romeo, that did spit his body
Upon a rapier's point. Stay, Tybalt, stay !
Romeo, I come ! this do I drink to thee.   58
   [She falls upon her bed within the curtains.]

*

   Enter Lady of the House and Nurse.   IV, iv

LADY
   Hold, take these keys and fetch more spices, nurse.

NURSE
   They call for dates and quinces in the pastry.
      Enter old Capulet.

CAPULET
   Come, stir, stir, stir ! The second cock hath crowed,
   The curfew bell hath rung, 'tis three o'clock.
   Look to the baked meats, good Angelica ;   5
   Spare not for cost.

NURSE   Go, you cot-quean, go,   6
   Get you to bed ! Faith, you'll be sick to-morrow
   For this night's watching.   8

---

47 *mandrakes* mandragora (a narcotic plant with a forked root resembling the human form, supposed to utter maddening shrieks when uprooted) **58** s.d. (from Q1)
IV, iv Within Capulet's house **5** *baked meats* meat pies **6** *cot-quean* a man who plays housewife **8** *watching* staying awake

CAPULET

No, not a whit. What, I have watched ere now
All night for lesser cause, and ne'er been sick.

LADY

11   Ay, you have been a mouse-hunt in your time;
But I will watch you from such watching now.

Exit Lady and Nurse.

CAPULET

13   A jealous hood, a jealous hood!

*Enter three or four [Fellows] with
spits and logs and baskets.*

                   Now, fellow,
What is there?

1. FELLOW

15   Things for the cook, sir; but I know not what.

CAPULET

Make haste, make haste.   *[Exit first Fellow.]*
                Sirrah, fetch drier logs.
Call Peter; he will show thee where they are.

2. FELLOW

18   I have a head, sir, that will find out logs
And never trouble Peter for the matter.

CAPULET

20   Mass, and well said; a merry whoreson, ha!

21   Thou shalt be loggerhead.

[Exit second Fellow, with the others.]
            Good Father! 'tis day.
The County will be here with music straight,
For so he said he would.

Play music.   I hear him near.
Nurse! Wife! What, ho! What, nurse, I say!

---

11 *mouse-hunt* i.e. a nocturnal prowler after women   13 *A jealous hood* you wear the cap (or hood) of jealousy   15, 18 *1. Fellow, 2. Fellow* (Q2 reads 'Fellow' in both instances)   18 *I . . . logs* i.e. my head is wooden and has an affinity for logs   20 *Mass* by the Mass; *whoreson* bastard, rascal   21 *loggerhead* blockhead

Enter Nurse.

Go waken Juliet ; go and trim her up.   25
I'll go and chat with Paris. Hie, make haste,
Make haste ! The bridegroom he is come already :
Make haste, I say.   *[Exit.]*
  [Nurse goes to curtains.]   IV, v

NURSE

Mistress ! what, mistress ! Juliet ! Fast, I warrant her, she.   1
Why, lamb ! why, lady ! Fie, you slug-abed.   2
Why, love, I say ! madam ! sweetheart ! Why, bride !
What, not a word ? You take your pennyworths now ;   4
Sleep for a week ; for the next night, I warrant,
The County Paris hath set up his rest   6
That you shall rest but little. God forgive me !
Marry, and amen. How sound is she asleep !
I needs must wake her. Madam, madam, madam !
Ay, let the County take you in your bed ;
He'll fright you up, i' faith. Will it not be ?
  [Draws aside the curtains.]
What, dressed, and in your clothes, and down again ?   12
I must needs wake you. Lady ! lady ! lady !
Alas, alas ! Help, help ! my lady 's dead !
O weraday that ever I was born !   15
Some aqua vitae, ho ! My lord ! my lady !   16
  [Enter Mother.]

MOTHER

What noise is here ?

NURSE   O lamentable day !

MOTHER

What is the matter ?

NURSE   Look, look ! O heavy day !

---

25 *trim her up* dress her neatly
IV, v 1 *Fast* fast asleep **2** *slug-abed* sleepyhead **4** *pennyworths* small
portions **6** *set . . . rest* i.e. made his firm decision (from primero, a card
game) **12** *down* back to bed **15** *weraday* welladay, alas **16** *aqua vitae*
alcoholic spirits

MOTHER
> O me, O me! My child, my only life!
20 > Revive, look up, or I will die with thee!
> Help, help! Call help.
>> *Enter Father.*

FATHER
> For shame, bring Juliet forth; her lord is come.

NURSE
> She's dead, deceased; she's dead, alack the day!

MOTHER
> Alack the day, she's dead, she's dead, she's dead!

CAPULET
> Ha! let me see her. Out alas! she's cold,
> Her blood is settled, and her joints are stiff;
> Life and these lips have long been separated.
> Death lies on her like an untimely frost
> Upon the sweetest flower of all the field.

NURSE
30 > O lamentable day!

MOTHER   O woeful time!

CAPULET
> Death, that hath ta'en her hence to make me wail,
> Ties up my tongue and will not let me speak.
>> *Enter Friar [Laurence] and the County [Paris, with*
>> *Musicians].*

FRIAR
> Come, is the bride ready to go to church?

CAPULET
> Ready to go, but never to return.
> O son, the night before thy wedding day
> Hath Death lain with thy wife. There she lies,
> Flower as she was, deflowerèd by him.
> Death is my son-in-law, Death is my heir;
> My daughter he hath wedded. I will die
> And leave him all. Life, living, all is Death's.

PARIS
> Have I thought long to see this morning's face,

And doth it give me such a sight as this?

MOTHER
Accursed, unhappy, wretched, hateful day!
Most miserable hour that e'er time saw
In lasting labor of his pilgrimage!   45
But one, poor one, one poor and loving child,   46
But one thing to rejoice and solace in,
And cruel Death hath catched it from my sight.

NURSE
O woe! O woeful, woeful, woeful day!
Most lamentable day, most woeful day
That ever ever I did yet behold!
O day, O day, O day! O hateful day!
Never was seen so black a day as this.
O woeful day! O woeful day!

PARIS
Beguiled, divorcèd, wrongèd, spited, slain!
Most detestable Death, by thee beguiled,
By cruel cruel thee quite overthrown.
O love! O life! not life, but love in death!

CAPULET
Despised, distressèd, hated, martyred, killed!
Uncomfortable time, why cam'st thou now
To murder, murder our solemnity?   61
O child, O child! my soul, and not my child!
Dead art thou – alack, my child is dead,
And with my child my joys are burièd!

FRIAR
Peace, ho, for shame! Confusion's cure lives not
In these confusions. Heaven and yourself
Had part in this fair maid – now heaven hath all,
And all the better is it for the maid.
Your part in her you could not keep from death,   69
But heaven keeps his part in eternal life.   70

---

45 *lasting labor* continuous toil   **46** *But one* (cf. III, v, 166)   **61** *To murder
. . . solemnity* to spoil our ceremony   **69** *Your part* her mortal body, gener-
ated by her parents   **70** *his part* her immortal soul, created directly by God

The most you sought was her promotion,
For 'twas your heaven she should be advanced;
And weep ye now, seeing she is advanced
Above the clouds, as high as heaven itself?
O, in this love, you love your child so ill
That you run mad, seeing that she is well.
She's not well married that lives married long,
But she's best married that dies married young.

79   Dry up your tears and stick your rosemary
On this fair corse, and, as the custom is,
In all her best array bear her to church;
82   For though fond nature bids us all lament,
83   Yet nature's tears are reason's merriment.

CAPULET
All things that we ordainèd festival
Turn from their office to black funeral –
Our instruments to melancholy bells,
Our wedding cheer to a sad burial feast;
Our solemn hymns to sullen dirges change;
Our bridal flowers serve for a buried corse;
And all things change them to the contrary.

FRIAR
Sir, go you in; and, madam, go with him;
And go, Sir Paris. Every one prepare
To follow this fair corse unto her grave.
94   The heavens do low'r upon you for some ill;
95   Move them no more by crossing their high will.
          Exeunt [casting rosemary on her and shutting the
          curtains]. Manet [the Nurse with Musicians].

1. MUSICIAN
Faith, we may put up our pipes and be gone.

NURSE
Honest good fellows, ah, put up, put up!
98   For well you know this is a pitiful case.   *[Exit.]*

79 *rosemary* plant symbolizing remembrance   82 *fond nature* foolish human
nature   83 *merriment* cause for optimism   94 *low'r* look angrily; *ill* sin
95 s.d. *casting . . . curtains* (from Q1)   98 s.d. (Q2 reads 'Exit omnes.')

1 . MUSICIAN
    Ay, by my troth, the case may be amended.   99
      Enter Peter.

PETER Musicians, O, musicians, 'Heart's ease,' 'Heart's   100
    ease'! O, an you will have me live, play 'Heart's ease.'

1 . MUSICIAN Why 'Heart's ease'?

PETER O, musicians, because my heart itself plays 'My   103
    heart is full of woe.' O, play me some merry dump to   04
    comfort me.

1 . MUSICIAN Not a dump we! 'Tis no time to play now.

PETER You will not then?

1 . MUSICIAN No.

PETER I will then give it you soundly.

1 . MUSICIAN What will you give us?

PETER No money, on my faith, but the gleek. I will give   111
    you the minstrel.

1 . MUSICIAN Then will I give you the serving-creature.

PETER Then will I lay the serving-creature's dagger on
    your pate. I will carry no crotchets. I'll re you, I'll fa   115
    you. Do you note me?

1 . MUSICIAN An you re us and fa us, you note us.

2 . MUSICIAN Pray you put up your dagger, and put out   118
    your wit.

PETER Then have at you with my wit! I will dry-beat you   120
    with an iron wit, and put up my iron dagger. Answer
    me like men.

      'When griping grief the heart doth wound,   123
        And doleful dumps the mind oppress,
      Then music with her silver sound' –

---

99 *case* instrument case; *amended* repaired; *s.d. Enter Peter* (Q2 has 'Enter
Will Kemp,' the actor playing Peter's role)   **100, 103–04** *Heart's ease, My
heart is full of woe* (old ballad tunes)   **104** *dump* slow dance melody   **111**
gleek mock   **111–12** *give you* insultingly call you   **115** *carry* put up with;
crotchets (1) whims, (2) quarter notes in music; *re, fa* (musical notes)   **118**
put out display   **120** *Then . . . wit* (added to preceding speech in Q2); *dry-
beat* thrash   **123–25** (The second line is missing in Q2 but appears in Q1.
The song is from Richard Edwards' 'In Commendation of Music,' in *The
Paradise of Dainty Devices*, 1576.)

Why 'silver sound'? Why 'music with her silver sound'?
127   What say you, Simon Catling?
1 . MUSICIAN Marry, sir, because silver hath a sweet
sound.
129 PETER Pretty! What say you, Hugh Rebeck?
2 . MUSICIAN I say 'silver sound' because musicians
sound for silver.
132 PETER Pretty too! What say you, James Soundpost?
3 . MUSICIAN Faith, I know not what to say.
134 PETER O, I cry you mercy! you are the singer. I will say
for you. It is 'music with her silver sound' because
musicians have no gold for sounding.
          'Then music with her silver sound
                    With speedy help doth lend redress.'   *Exit.*
1 . MUSICIAN What a pestilent knave is this same!
2 . MUSICIAN Hang him, Jack! Come, we'll in here, tarry
141   for the mourners, and stay dinner.   *Exit [with others].*

*

V, i   *Enter Romeo.*
ROMEO
1   If I may trust the flattering truth of sleep,
          My dreams presage some joyful news at hand.
3   My bosom's lord sits lightly in his throne,
          And all this day an unaccustomed spirit
          Lifts me above the ground with cheerful thoughts.
          I dreamt my lady came and found me dead
          (Strange dream that gives a dead man leave to think!)
          And breathed such life with kisses in my lips
          That I revived and was an emperor.
          Ah me! how sweet is love itself possessed,
11   When but love's shadows are so rich in joy!

---

127 *Catling* (lutestring)   129 *Rebeck* (three-stringed fiddle)   132 *Soundpost* (wooden peg in a violin, supporting the bridge)   134 *cry you mercy* beg your pardon   141 *stay* await
V, i A street in Mantua   1 *flattering* favorable to me; *truth of sleep* (cf. I, iv, 52)   3 *bosom's lord* heart   11 *shadows* dream-images

Enter Romeo's man [Balthasar, booted].
News from Verona ! How now, Balthasar ?
Dost thou not bring me letters from the friar ?
How doth my lady ? Is my father well ?
How fares my Juliet ? That I ask again,
For nothing can be ill if she be well.

MAN
  Then she is well, and nothing can be ill.
  Her body sleeps in Capel's monument,
  And her immortal part with angels lives.
  I saw her laid low in her kindred's vault
  And presently took post to tell it you.   21
  O, pardon me for bringing these ill news,
  Since you did leave it for my office, sir.

ROMEO
  Is it e'en so ? Then I defy you, stars !   24
  Thou knowest my lodging. Get me ink and paper
  And hire posthorses. I will hence to-night.

MAN
  I do beseech you, sir, have patience.
  Your looks are pale and wild and do import   28
  Some misadventure.

ROMEO   Tush, thou art deceived.
  Leave me and do the thing I bid thee do.
  Hast thou no letters to me from the friar ?

MAN
  No, my good lord.

ROMEO   No matter. Get thee gone
  And hire those horses. I'll be with thee straight.
                                        Exit [Balthasar].

  Well, Juliet, I will lie with thee to-night.
  Let's see for means. O mischief, thou art swift
  To enter in the thoughts of desperate men !
  I do remember an apothecary,
  And hereabouts 'a dwells, which late I noted

21 *presently* at once; *took post* hired posthorses   24 *stars* (cf. I, iv, 107)   28
import suggest

39　In tatt'red weeds, with overwhelming brows,
40　Culling of simples. Meagre were his looks,
　　Sharp misery had worn him to the bones;
　　And in his needy shop a tortoise hung,
　　An alligator stuffed, and other skins
　　Of ill-shaped fishes; and about his shelves
45　A beggarly account of empty boxes,
　　Green earthen pots, bladders, and musty seeds,
47　Remnants of packthread, and old cakes of roses
　　Were thinly scatterèd, to make up a show.
　　Noting this penury, to myself I said,
　　'An if a man did need a poison now
　　Whose sale is present death in Mantua,
52　Here lives a caitiff wretch would sell it him.'
　　O, this same thought did but forerun my need,
　　And this same needy man must sell it me.
　　As I remember, this should be the house.
　　Being holiday, the beggar's shop is shut.
　　What, ho! apothecary!
　　　　　[Enter Apothecary.]
APOTHECARY　　　　Who calls so loud?
ROMEO
　　Come hither, man. I see that thou art poor.
　　Hold, there is forty ducats. Let me have
60　A dram of poison, such soon-speeding gear
　　As will disperse itself through all the veins
　　That the life-weary taker may fall dead,
　　And that the trunk may be discharged of breath
　　As violently as hasty powder fired
65　Doth hurry from the fatal cannon's womb.
APOTHECARY
66　Such mortal drugs I have; but Mantua's law
67　Is death to any he that utters them.

---

39 *weeds* garments; *overwhelming* overhanging　**40** *simples* herbs　**45** *account* quantity　**47** *cakes of roses* compressed rose petals, used for perfume　**52** *caitiff* miserable　**60** *gear* stuff　**65** *womb* i.e. barrel　**66** *mortal* deadly　**67** *utters* gives out

ROMEO
Art thou so bare and full of wretchedness
And fearest to die ? Famine is in thy cheeks,
Need and oppression starveth in thy eyes,   70
Contempt and beggary hangs upon thy back :
The world is not thy friend, nor the world's law ;
The world affords no law to make thee rich ;
Then be not poor, but break it and take this.

APOTHECARY
My poverty but not my will consents.

ROMEO
I pay thy poverty and not thy will.

APOTHECARY
Put this in any liquid thing you will
And drink it off, and if you had the strength
Of twenty men, it would dispatch you straight.

ROMEO
There is thy gold – worse poison to men's souls,
Doing more murder in this loathsome world,
Than these poor compounds that thou mayst not sell.
I sell thee poison ; thou hast sold me none.
Farewell. Buy food and get thyself in flesh.
Come, cordial and not poison, go with me
To Juliet's grave ; for there must I use thee.   *Exeunt.*

*

Enter Friar John to Friar Laurence.   V, ii

JOHN
Holy Franciscan friar, brother, ho !
    Enter [Friar] Laurence.

LAURENCE
This same should be the voice of Friar John.
Welcome from Mantua. What says Romeo ?
Or, if his mind be writ, give me his letter.

70 *starveth* are revealed by the starved look
V, ii Friar Laurence's cell

JOHN

5   Going to find a barefoot brother out,
6   One of our order, to associate me
       Here in this city visiting the sick,
8   And finding him, the searchers of the town,
       Suspecting that we both were in a house
10   Where the infectious pestilence did reign,
       Sealed up the doors, and would not let us forth,
       So that my speed to Mantua there was stayed.

LAURENCE

       Who bare my letter, then, to Romeo ?

JOHN

       I could not send it – here it is again –
       Nor get a messenger to bring it thee,
       So fearful were they of infection.

LAURENCE

17   Unhappy fortune ! By my brotherhood,
18   The letter was not nice, but full of charge,
       Of dear import ; and the neglecting it
       May do much danger. Friar John, go hence,
21   Get me an iron crow and bring it straight
       Unto my cell.

JOHN   Brother, I'll go and bring it thee.   *Exit*.

LAURENCE

       Now must I to the monument alone.
       Within this three hours will fair Juliet wake.
25   She will beshrew me much that Romeo
26   Hath had no notice of these accidents ;
       But I will write again to Mantua,
       And keep her at my cell till Romeo come –
       Poor living corse, closed in a dead man's tomb !   *Exit*

*

5 *a barefoot brother* another friar   6 *associate* accompany   8 *searchers*
health officers   10 *pestilence* plague   17 *brotherhood* order (Franciscans)
18 *nice* trivial; *charge* important matters   21 *crow* crowbar   25 *beshrew*
reprove   26 *accidents* occurrences

Enter Paris and his Page [with flowers and sweet   **V, iii**
water].

PARIS

Give me thy torch, boy. Hence, and stand aloof.
Yet put it out, for I would not be seen.
Under yond yew tree lay thee all along,   3
Holding thy ear close to the hollow ground.
So shall no foot upon the churchyard tread
(Being loose, unfirm, with digging up of graves)
But thou shalt hear it. Whistle then to me,
As signal that thou hearest something approach.
Give me those flowers. Do as I bid thee, go.

PAGE *[aside]*

I am almost afraid to stand alone
Here in the churchyard; yet I will adventure. *[Retires.]*

PARIS

Sweet flower, with flowers thy bridal bed I strew
(O woe! thy canopy is dust and stones)
Which with sweet water nightly I will dew;
Or, wanting that, with tears distilled by moans.
The obsequies that I for thee will keep
Nightly shall be to strew thy grave and weep.
Whistle Boy.
The boy gives warning something doth approach.
What cursèd foot wanders this way to-night
To cross my obsequies and true love's rite?   20
What, with a torch? Muffle me, night, awhile. *[Retires.]* 21
Enter Romeo [and Balthasar with a torch, a mattock,
and a crow of iron].

ROMEO

Give me that mattock and the wrenching iron.
Hold, take this letter. Early in the morning
See thou deliver it to my lord and father.

V, iii A churchyard in Verona **s.d.** *with . . . water* (from Q1); *sweet* per-
fumed **3** *all along* at full length **20** *cross* interfere with **21 s.d.** *and
Balthasar . . . iron* (from Q1; Q2 reads 'Enter Romeo and Peter.'); *mattock*
pickaxe

Give me the light. Upon thy life I charge thee,
Whate'er thou hearest or seest, stand all aloof
And do not interrupt me in my course.
Why I descend into this bed of death
Is partly to behold my lady's face,
But chiefly to take thence from her dead finger
31   A precious ring – a ring that I must use
In dear employment. Therefore hence, be gone.
33   But if thou, jealous, dost return to pry
In what I farther shall intend to do,
By heaven, I will tear thee joint by joint
And strew this hungry churchyard with thy limbs.
The time and my intents are savage-wild,
More fierce and more inexorable far
Than empty tigers or the roaring sea.

BALTHASAR
I will be gone, sir, and not trouble you.

ROMEO
41   So shalt thou show me friendship. Take thou that.
Live, and be prosperous ; and farewell, good fellow.

BALTHASAR [aside]
For all this same, I'll hide me hereabout.
His looks I fear, and his intents I doubt.   [Retires.]

ROMEO
Thou detestable maw, thou womb of death,
Gorged with the dearest morsel of the earth,
Thus I enforce thy rotten jaws to open,
48   And in despite I'll cram thee with more food.
    [Romeo opens the tomb.]

PARIS
This is that banished haughty Montague
That murd'red my love's cousin – with which grief
It is supposèd the fair creature died –

---

31 *A precious ring* (a false excuse to assure Balthasar's non-interference)   33
jealous curious, jealous of my privacy   41 *that* (a purse)   48 *in despite* to
spite you; s.d. (from Q1)

And here is come to do some villainous shame
To the dead bodies. I will apprehend him.   53
Stop thy unhallowèd toil, vile Montague!
Can vengeance be pursued further than death?
Condemnèd villain, I do apprehend thee.
Obey, and go with me; for thou must die.

ROMEO

I must indeed; and therefore came I hither.
Good gentle youth, tempt not a desp'rate man.   60
Fly hence and leave me. Think upon these gone;
Let them affright thee. I beseech thee, youth,
Put not another sin upon my head
By urging me to fury. O, be gone!
By heaven, I love thee better than myself,
For I come hither armed against myself.
Stay not, be gone. Live, and hereafter say
A madman's mercy bid thee run away.

PARIS   68

I do defy thy conjuration
And apprehend thee for a felon here.

ROMEO

Wilt thou provoke me? Then have at thee, boy!
      [They fight.]

PAGE

O Lord, they fight! I will go call the watch.
                              [Exit. Paris falls.]

PARIS

O, I am slain! If thou be merciful,
Open the tomb, lay me with Juliet.   [Dies.]

ROMEO

In faith, I will. Let me peruse this face.   74
Mercutio's kinsman, noble County Paris!
What said my man when my betossèd soul
Did not attend him as we rode? I think   77

53 *apprehend* arrest 60 *gone* dead 68 *conjuration* threatening appeal
74 *peruse* read, look at 77 *attend* pay attention to

He told me Paris should have married Juliet.
Said he not so? or did I dream it so?
Or am I mad, hearing him talk of Juliet,
To think it was so? O, give me thy hand,
One writ with me in sour misfortune's book!
I'll bury thee in a triumphant grave.

84 A grave? O, no, a lanthorn, slaught'red youth,
For here lies Juliet, and her beauty makes
86 This vault a feasting presence full of light.
Death, lie thou there, by a dead man interred.
[Lays him in the tomb.]
How oft when men are at the point of death
89 Have they been merry! which their keepers call
90 A lightning before death. O, how may I
Call this a lightning? O my love! my wife!
Death, that hath sucked the honey of thy breath,
Hath had no power yet upon thy beauty.
94 Thou are not conquered. Beauty's ensign yet
Is crimson in thy lips and in thy cheeks,
And death's pale flag is not advancèd there.
Tybalt, liest thou there in thy bloody sheet?
O, what more favor can I do to thee
Than with that hand that cut thy youth in twain
To sunder his that was thine enemy?
Forgive me, cousin! Ah, dear Juliet,
102 Why art thou yet so fair? Shall I believe
That unsubstantial Death is amorous,
And that the lean abhorrèd monster keeps
Thee here in dark to be his paramour?
For fear of that I still will stay with thee
And never from this pallet of dim night

---

84 *lanthorn* lantern (a many-windowed turret room)   86 *presence* presence
chamber   89 *keepers* jailers   90 *A lightning before death* (a common phrase
for the phenomenon described)   94 *ensign* banner   102 *Why . . . fair*
(followed in Q2 by a superfluous 'I will believe,' evidently another manuscript cancellation printed in error)

Depart again. Here, here will I remain   108
With worms that are thy chambermaids. O, here
Will I set up my everlasting rest   110
And shake the yoke of inauspicious stars   111
From this world-wearied flesh. Eyes, look your last!
Arms, take your last embrace! and, lips, O you
The doors of breath, seal with a righteous kiss
A dateless bargain to engrossing death!   115
Come, bitter conduct; come, unsavory guide!   116
Thou desperate pilot, now at once run on   117
The dashing rocks thy seasick weary bark!   118
Here's to my love! *[Drinks.]* O true apothecary!   119
Thy drugs are quick. Thus with a kiss I die.
    [Falls.]
    Enter Friar [Laurence], with lanthorn, crow, and spade.

FRIAR

Saint Francis be my speed! how oft to-night   121
Have my old feet stumbled at graves! Who's there?   122

BALTHASAR

Here's one, a friend, and one that knows you well.

FRIAR

Bliss be upon you! Tell me, good my friend,
What torch is yond that vainly lends his light
To grubs and eyeless skulls? As I discern,
It burneth in the Capels' monument.

BALTHASAR

It doth so, holy sir; and there's my master,
One that you love.

---

108 *again. Here* (Q2 prints between these words the following material, obviously cancelled in the manuscript because it appears in substance later in the speech: 'come lie thou in my arm. Here's to thy health, where e'er thou tumblest in. O true Apothecary! Thy drugs are quick. Thus with a kiss I die. Depart again.') 110 *set . . . rest* make my decision to stay forever (cf. IV, v, 6) 111 *inauspicious stars* (cf. V, i, 24) 115 *dateless* in perpetuity; *engrossing* taking everything 116 *conduct* guide, i.e. the poison 117 *pilot* i.e. Romeo's soul 118 *bark* i.e. Romeo's body 119 *Here's to my love* (cf. IV, iii, 58) 121 *speed* aid 122 *stumbled at graves* (a bad omen)

FRIAR   Who is it?
BALTHASAR   Romeo.
FRIAR
How long hath he been there?
BALTHASAR   Full half an hour.
FRIAR
Go with me to the vault.
BALTHASAR   I dare not, sir.
My master knows not but I am gone hence,
And fearfully did menace me with death
If I did stay to look on his intents.
FRIAR
Stay then, I'll go alone. Fear comes upon me.
136   O, much I fear some ill unthrifty thing.
BALTHASAR
As I did sleep under this yew tree here,
I dreamt my master and another fought,
And that my master slew him.
FRIAR   Romeo!
Alack, alack, what blood is this which stains
The stony entrance of this sepulchre?
What mean these masterless and gory swords
To lie discolored by this place of peace?
        [Enters the tomb.]
Romeo! O, pale! Who else? What, Paris too?
And steeped in blood? Ah, what an unkind hour
Is guilty of this lamentable chance!
The lady stirs.
        [Juliet rises.]
JULIET
148   O comfortable friar! where is my lord?
I do remember well where I should be,
And there I am. Where is my Romeo?
FRIAR
I hear some noise. Lady, come from that nest

136 *unthrifty* unfortunate   **148** *comfortable* comfort-giving

Of death, contagion, and unnatural sleep.
A greater power than we can contradict
Hath thwarted our intents. Come, come away.
Thy husband in thy bosom there lies dead;
And Paris too. Come, I'll dispose of thee
Among a sisterhood of holy nuns.
Stay not to question, for the watch is coming.
Come, go, good Juliet. I dare no longer stay.

JULIET
Go, get thee hence, for I will not away.   *Exit [Friar].*
What's here? A cup, closed in my true love's hand?
Poison, I see, hath been his timeless end.   162
O churl! drunk all, and left no friendly drop
To help me after? I will kiss thy lips.
Haply some poison yet doth hang on them
To make me die with a restorative.   166
        [Kisses him.]
Thy lips are warm!

CHIEF WATCHMAN *[within]* Lead, boy. Which way?

JULIET
Yea, noise? Then I'll be brief. O happy dagger!   169
        [Snatches Romeo's dagger.]
This is thy sheath; there rust, and let me die.   170
        [She stabs herself and falls.]
        Enter [Paris's] Boy and Watch.

BOY
This is the place. There, where the torch doth burn.

CHIEF WATCHMAN
The ground is bloody. Search about the churchyard.
Go, some of you; whoe'er you find attach.
                        [Exeunt some of the Watch.]
Pitiful sight! here lies the County slain;
And Juliet bleeding, warm, and newly dead,
Who here hath lain this two days burièd.
Go, tell the Prince; run to the Capulets;

162 *timeless* untimely   **166** *restorative* i.e. restoring me to you   **169** *happy*
opportune   **170** *rust* (Q1 'rest')

Raise up the Montagues ; some others search.
                    [Exeunt others of the Watch.]

We see the ground whereon these woes do lie,

180   But the true ground of all these piteous woes

181   We cannot without circumstance descry.
          *Enter [some of the Watch, with] Romeo's Man
          [Balthasar].*

2. WATCHMAN
Here's Romeo's man. We found him in the churchyard.

CHIEF WATCHMAN
Hold him in safety till the Prince come hither.
          Enter Friar [Laurence] and another Watchman.

3. WATCHMAN
Here is a friar that trembles, sighs, and weeps.
We took this mattock and this spade from him
As he was coming from this churchyard side.

CHIEF WATCHMAN
A great suspicion ! Stay the friar too.
          Enter the Prince [and Attendants].

PRINCE
What misadventure is so early up,

189   That calls our person from our morning rest ?
          Enter Capulet and his Wife [with others].

CAPULET
What should it be, that is so shrieked abroad ?

WIFE
O the people in the street cry 'Romeo,'
Some 'Juliet,' and some 'Paris' ; and all run,
With open outcry, toward our monument.

PRINCE
What fear is this which startles in your ears ?

CHIEF WATCHMAN
Sovereign, here lies the County Paris slain ;
And Romeo dead ; and Juliet, dead before,
Warm and new killed.

---

180 *ground* basis   **181** *circumstance* details   **189** s.d. *Enter . . . Wife* (in Q2
'Enter Capels' appears here, with the present stage direction after l. 201)

PRINCE
>Search, seek, and know how this foul murder comes.

CHIEF WATCHMAN
>Here is a friar, and slaughtered Romeo's man,
>With instruments upon them fit to open
>These dead men's tombs.

CAPULET
>O heavens! O wife, look how our daughter bleeds!
>This dagger hath mista'en, for, lo, his house   203
>Is empty on the back of Montague,
>And it missheathèd in my daughter's bosom!

WIFE
>O me! this sight of death is as a bell
>That warns my old age to a sepulchre.   207
>>*Enter Montague [and others].*

PRINCE
>Come, Montague; for thou art early up
>To see thy son and heir more early down.

MONTAGUE
>Alas, my liege, my wife is dead to-night!
>Grief of my son's exile hath stopped her breath.
>What further woe conspires against mine age?

PRINCE
>Look, and thou shalt see.

MONTAGUE
>O thou untaught! what manners is in this,
>To press before thy father to a grave?

PRINCE
>Seal up the mouth of outrage for a while,   216
>Till we can clear these ambiguities
>And know their spring, their head, their true descent;
>And then will I be general of your woes   219
>And lead you even to death. Meantime forbear,   220

---

203 *his house* its sheath **207** *my old age* (she is only twenty-eight – I, iii, 72-73 – but she feels old and ready for death; cf. III, ii, 89) **216** *mouth of outrage* violent outcries **219** *general . . . woes* your leader in lamentation **220** *even to death* even if grief kills us

And let mischance be slave to patience.
Bring forth the parties of suspicion.

FRIAR

I am the greatest, able to do least,
Yet most suspected, as the time and place
Doth make against me, of this direful murder;
226 And here I stand, both to impeach and purge
Myself condemnèd and myself excused.

PRINCE

Then say at once what thou dost know in this.

FRIAR

229 I will be brief, for my short date of breath
Is not so long as is a tedious tale.
Romeo, there dead, was husband to that Juliet;
And she, there dead, that Romeo's faithful wife.
I married them; and their stol'n marriage day
Was Tybalt's doomsday, whose untimely death
Banished the new-made bridegroom from this city;
For whom, and not for Tybalt, Juliet pined.
You, to remove that siege of grief from her,
238 Betrothed and would have married her perforce
To County Paris. Then comes she to me
And with wild looks bid me devise some mean
To rid her from this second marriage,
Or in my cell there would she kill herself.
Then gave I her (so tutored by my art)
A sleeping potion; which so took effect
As I intended, for it wrought on her
The form of death. Meantime I writ to Romeo
247 That he should hither come as this dire night
To help to take her from her borrowèd grave,
Being the time the potion's force should cease.
But he which bore my letter, Friar John,
Was stayed by accident, and yesternight
Returned my letter back. Then all alone

---

226 *impeach and purge* accuse and exonerate   229 *date of breath* life expectancy   238 *perforce* by force   247 *as* on

At the prefixèd hour of her waking
Came I to take her from her kindred's vault;
Meaning to keep her closely at my cell   255
Till I conveniently could send to Romeo.
But when I came, some minute ere the time
Of her awakening, here untimely lay
The noble Paris and true Romeo dead.
She wakes; and I entreated her come forth
And bear this work of heaven with patience;
But then a noise did scare me from the tomb,
And she, too desperate, would not go with me,
But, as it seems, did violence on herself.
All this I know, and to the marriage
Her nurse is privy; and if aught in this   266
Miscarried by my fault, let my old life
Be sacrificed, some hour before his time,
Unto the rigor of severest law.

PRINCE
We still have known thee for a holy man.   270
Where's Romeo's man? What can he say in this?

BALTHASAR
I brought my master news of Juliet's death;
And then in post he came from Mantua
To this same place, to this same monument.
This letter he early bid me give his father,
And threat'ned me with death, going in the vault,
If I departed not and left him there.

PRINCE
Give me the letter. I will look on it.
Where is the County's page that raised the watch?
Sirrah, what made your master in this place?   280

BOY
He came with flowers to strew his lady's grave;
And bid me stand aloof, and so I did.
Anon comes one with light to ope the tomb;   283

255 *closely* secretly   266 *privy* in the secret   270 *still* always   280 *made*
did   283 *Anon* soon

284   And by and by my master drew on him ;
        And then I ran away to call the watch.

PRINCE
        This letter doth make good the friar's words,
        Their course of love, the tidings of her death ;
        And here he writes that he did buy a poison
        Of a poor pothecary, and therewithal
        Came to this vault to die, and lie with Juliet.
        Where be these enemies ? Capulet, Montague,
        See what a scourge is laid upon your hate,
293   That heaven finds means to kill your joys with love.
294   And I, for winking at your discords too,
        Have lost a brace of kinsmen. All are punished.

CAPULET
        O brother Montague, give me thy hand.
297   This is my daughter's jointure, for no more
        Can I demand.

MONTAGUE   But I can give thee more ;
        For I will raise her statue in pure gold,
        That whiles Verona by that name is known,
301   There shall no figure at such rate be set
        As that of true and faithful Juliet.

CAPULET
        As rich shall Romeo's by his lady's lie –
        Poor sacrifices of our enmity !

PRINCE
305   A glooming peace this morning with it brings.
        The sun for sorrow will not show his head.
        Go hence, to have more talk of these sad things ;
        Some shall be pardoned, and some punishèd ;
        For never was a story of more woe
        Than this of Juliet and her Romeo.   *[Exeunt omnes.]*

---

284 *by and by* almost at once; *drew* drew his sword   **293** *with* by means of **294** *winking at* shutting my eyes to   **297** *jointure* marriage portion   **301** *rate* value   **305** *glooming* cloudy, overcast

APPENDIX:
DEPARTURES FROM THE
1599 QUARTO

The only departures from the copy-text (second quarto, 1599) are listed below, except for relineations, corrections of obvious typographical errors, added stage directions (in brackets), and the treatment of cancelled passages (explained in the notes). Variants in speech prefixes within a scene have been regularized without comment. All the listed readings have been adopted from the first quarto, 1597, except those marked Q3 (third quarto, 1609), Q4 (fourth quarto, n.d.), F1 (first folio, 1623), F2 (second folio, 1632), F4 (fourth folio, 1683), and Eds (emendation, usually made quite early in the history of Shakespearean textual study and still generally accepted by modern editors). The adopted reading in italics is followed by the reading of the copy-text in roman.

I, i, 21 *cruel* (Q4) civil 26 *in sense* sense 30 *comes two* comes 60 *swashing* (Q4) washing 85 *mistemp'red* mistemperèd 118 *drave* (F1) drive 151 *sun* (Eds) same 175 *create* created 177 *well-seeming* well-seeing 188 *raised* made 190 *lovers'* loving 200 *Bid a sick* A sick *make* makes 201 *Ah* A 209 *unharmed* uncharmed 216 *makes* (Q4) make

I, ii, 32 *on more view* (Q4) one more view 70 *and Livia* Livia

I, iii, 66, 67 *honor* hour 99 *make it fly* make fly

I, iv, 39 *done* dum 42 *Of this sir-reverence* Or save your reverence 45 *like lamps* lights lights 47 *five wits* fine wits 66 *maid* man 72 *O'er courtiers'* On courtiers 81 *dreams he* he dreams 113 *sail* suit

I, v, 18 *Ah ha* Ah 95 *ready* did ready

II, i, 10 *pronounce* prouaunt *dove* day 12 *heir* her 38 *et cetera,* or

II, ii, 31 *pacing* puffing   41 *nor any other part* (omitted in Q2)   44 *name* word   83 *washed* (F2) washeth   99 *havior* behavior   101 *more cunning* coying   110 *circled* circle   153 *suit* (Q4) strife   163 *mine* (omitted in Q2)   168 *sweet* (F2) Neece   *At what* What   179 *her* his   189 *father's* friar's close

II, iii, 4 *fiery* burning   22 *sometime's* sometime   74 *ring yet* yet ringing   85 *She whom* Her

II, iv, 19 *I can tell you* (omitted in Q2)   28 *fantasticoes* fantasies   96 (spoken by Romeo in Q2)   97 (spoken by Mercutio in Q2)   109 *for* (omitted in Q2)   187 *I warrant* (F2) Warrant   197 *Ah* (Eds) A

II, v, 26 *have I had* (F2) have I

III, i, 106 *soundly too. Your* (Eds) soundly, to your   120 *Alive* He gan   122 *eyed* end   145 *O husband* (Eds) O cousin, husband   164 *agile* aged   186 *hate's* hearts

III, ii, 9 *By* (F2) And by   21 *he* (Q4) I   49 *the* (F2) thee   51 *determine of* (F1) determine   76 *Dove-feathered* (Eds) Ravenous dove-feathered   79 *damnèd* (F2) dimme

III, iii, 15 *Hence* Here   52 *Thou* Then   117 *lives* (F4) lies   138 *happy too* happy   143 *misbehaved* mishavèd   144 *pout'st upon* (Eds) puts up   163 *is* sir

III, iv, 34 *very very* very

III, v, 13 *exhales* exhale   83 *pardon him* (F2) pardon   182 *trained* liand

IV, i, 7 *talked* talk   45 *cure* care   46 *Ah* O   72 *slay* stay   83 *chapless* chapels   85 *his shroud* (Q4) his   98 *breath* breast   100 *wanny* (Eds) many   116 *waking* (Q3) walking

IV, iii, 58 *Romeo . . . thee* Romeo, Romeo, Romeo, here's drink, I drink to thee

IV, v, 41 *long* love   65 *cure* (Eds) care   81 *In all* And in   82 *fond* (F2) some   104 *full of woe* (Q4) full   129, 132 *Pretty* Prates

V, i, 15 *fares my* doth my Lady   24 *defy* deny   76 *pay* pray

V, iii, 3 *yew tree* young trees   68 *conjuration* commiration   137 *yew* (Q3) young   190 *shrieked* (Eds) shrike   209 *more early* now earling   232 *that* that's

SUPPLEMENTARY NOTE

III, ii, 49 *Or those eyes' shot that makes the answer 'I'*

Almost every editor since Capell except H. R. Hoppe (Crofts, 1943) has accepted his emendation *shut* for *shot*, reading "Or those eyes shut that make(s) thee answer 'I' [Ay]." Our copy-text, Q2, reads: "Or those eyes shot, that makes thee answer I." This reading is retained by the later quartos and folios, except that *thee* is emended to *the* in F2, F3, and F4.

I have supplied the apostrophe which makes *eyes* a possessive. Since Q2 regularly omits the apostrophe, as in "eyes windows" (IV, i, 100), supplying it does no violence to the text. *Shot* becomes a noun instead of a past participle. A usage similar to this appears in *Cymbeline*, I, i, 89–90, when Imogen says, "And I shall here abide the hourly shot / Of angry eyes."

If we interpret the passage as emended by Capell, Juliet refers to Romeo's eyes closed in death; or else she refers to the Nurse's eyes which, if shut, will indicate *ay*. If, as I think, the Nurse's eyes are meant, *shot* is the more logical reading. Juliet is studying the Nurse's face and may receive her answer from the Nurse's voice or, failing that, from the Nurse's eyes. Either form of affirmative, the spoken *ay* or the revelatory eye-glance (*eyes' shot*), will slay Juliet, who feels that her life is bound up with that of Romeo. As the eye-glance of the cockatrice (basilisk) darts death, so will the spoken *ay* or the eye-glance of the Nurse. This implies no malice on the part of the Nurse, since it is her message which may be fatal to Juliet.

Involved here is the Elizabethan theory of vision, or the act of seeing. It was believed that the eye darted forth a stream of very fine particles which pierced or fastened upon the beheld object and then relayed impulses back to the sender. The arrow was the appropriate image for such an eye-glance. Thus, Juliet promises her mother to look at Paris, "But no more deep will I endart mine eye" than her mother wishes (I, iii, 98). Such imagery is very common in the works of Shakespeare and his contemporaries.

If one retains *thee* as the correct reading, Juliet's meaning is as follows: "I am not myself if there be such a spoken *ay* or if there be your eye-glance that forces you to answer 'Ay.'" This makes sense after a fashion, but I have adopted the less tortuous reading of the later folios, changing *thee* to *the*. Juliet's meaning then becomes: "I am not myself if there be such a spoken *ay* or if there be your eye-glance that forms the answer 'Ay.'"

In support of the interpretation here given, we may notice that Mercutio pictures Romeo as being "dead," pierced by vision and by sound: "stabbed with a white wench's black eye; run through the ear with a love song" (II, iv, 14–15). So it is with Juliet. The spoken *ay* of the Nurse may slay her through the ear as effectively as the visual eye-dart of the cockatrice. Likewise, the Nurse's "eyes' shot," if it reveals the unspoken *ay*, will kill visually as effectively as her voice would kill through the ear.

FOR THE BEST IN PAPERBACKS, LOOK FOR THE

In every corner of the world, on every subject under the sun, Penguin represents quality and variety—the very best in publishing today.

For complete information about books available from Penguin—including Puffins, Penguin Classics, and Arkana—and how to order them, write to us at the appropriate address below. Please note that for copyright reasons the selection of books varies from country to country.

In the United Kingdom: Please write to *Dept. JC, Penguin Books Ltd, FREEPOST, West Drayton, Middlesex UB7 0BR.*

If you have any difficulty in obtaining a title, please send your order with the correct money, plus ten percent for postage and packaging, to *P.O. Box No. 11, West Drayton, Middlesex UB7 0BR*

In the United States: Please write to *Consumer Sales, Penguin USA, P.O. Box 999, Dept. 17109, Bergenfield, New Jersey 07621-0120.* VISA and MasterCard holders call 1-800-253-6476 to order all Penguin titles

In Canada: Please write to *Penguin Books Canada Ltd, 10 Alcorn Avenue, Suite 300, Toronto, Ontario M4V 3B2*

In Australia: Please write to *Penguin Books Australia Ltd, P.O. Box 257, Ringwood, Victoria 3134*

In New Zealand: Please write to *Penguin Books (NZ) Ltd, Private Bag 102902, North Shore Mail Centre, Auckland 10*

In India: Please write to *Penguin Books India Pvt Ltd, 706 Eros Apartments, 56 Nehru Place, New Delhi 110 019*

In the Netherlands: Please write to *Penguin Books Netherlands bv, Postbus 3507, NL-1001 AH Amsterdam*

In Germany: Please write to *Penguin Books Deutschland GmbH, Metzlerstrasse 26, 60594 Frankfurt am Main*

In Spain: Please write to *Penguin Books S. A., Bravo Murillo 19, 1° B, 28015 Madrid*

In Italy: Please write to *Penguin Italia s.r.l., Via Felice Casati 20, I-20124 Milano*

In France: Please write to *Penguin France S. A., 17 rue Lejeune, F-31000 Toulouse*

In Japan: Please write to *Penguin Books Japan, Ishikiribashi Building, 2-5-4, Suido, Bunkyo-ku, Tokyo 112*

In Greece: Please write to *Penguin Hellas Ltd, Dimocritou 3, GR-106 71 Athens*

In South Africa: Please write to *Longman Penguin Southern Africa (Pty) Ltd, Private Bag X08, Bertsham 2013*

The Pelican Shakespeare

The Penguin Shakespeare